Adve

# FEATURE SPOTLIGHT

This Week in Advertising...

**The Ad Man:**
Jason Reagert

**His New Campaign:**
Wedding bands—for the man who needs to get the ring on her finger...fast!

Maddox Communications has recently hired New York's golden boy, Jason Reagert. Rumors are flying that Maddox Communications may be going head-to-head with their chief rival, Golden Gate Promotions. The last thing Maddox needs is a scandal plaguing the pursuit, but it seems self-made, suave Jason Reagert is in quite the situation. Surely by now everyone has seen the notorious photo of one *Miss* Lauren Presley sporting quite the prominent baby bump. Seeing as how the mommy-to-be has just accepted the marriage proposal of Mr. Reagert...one can only assume she's marrying her baby's daddy.

Dear Reader,

Receiving an invitation to participate in a continuity series is such a thrill and honor for me! I especially enjoy the opportunity to work with other authors to build an exciting new story world—in this case, the world for KINGS OF THE BOARDROOM. In *Bossman's Baby Scandal,* it's my pleasure to introduce you to the driven men and women at Maddox Communications, an ad agency in scenic San Francisco.

Ambitious ad exec Jason Reagert expects a fresh start on the West Coast, a chance to make his mark outside his wealthy family's influence. But all too soon his ties back east tighten when he learns his ex-lover, Lauren Presley, is carrying his baby!

I hope you enjoy the glitz, glamour and high-powered dealings in KINGS OF THE BOARDROOM. I love to hear feedback from readers, so please feel free to contact me via my Web site, www.catherinemann.com, or write to me at P.O. Box 6065, Navarre, FL 32566.

Happy reading!

*Catherine*

# CATHERINE MANN

# BOSSMAN'S BABY SCANDAL

Published by Silhouette Books
**America's Publisher of Contemporary Romance**

If you purchased this book without a cover you should be aware that this book is stolen property. It was reported as "unsold and destroyed" to the publisher, and neither the author nor the publisher has received any payment for this "stripped book."

Special thanks and acknowledgment
to Catherine Mann for her contribution to the
KINGS OF THE BOARDROOM miniseries.

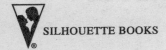

SILHOUETTE BOOKS

ISBN-13: 978-0-373-73001-8

BOSSMAN'S BABY SCANDAL

Copyright © 2010 by Harlequin Books S.A.

All rights reserved. Except for use in any review, the reproduction or utilization of this work in whole or in part in any form by any electronic, mechanical or other means, now known or hereafter invented, including xerography, photocopying and recording, or in any information storage or retrieval system, is forbidden without the written permission of the editorial office, Silhouette Books, 233 Broadway, New York, NY 10279 U.S.A.

This is a work of fiction. Names, characters, places and incidents are either the product of the author's imagination or are used fictitiously, and any resemblance to actual persons, living or dead, business establishments, events or locales is entirely coincidental.

This edition published by arrangement with Harlequin Books S.A.

® and TM are trademarks of Harlequin Books S.A., used under license. Trademarks indicated with ® are registered in the United States Patent and Trademark Office, the Canadian Trade Marks Office and in other countries.

Visit Silhouette Books at www.eHarlequin.com

**Printed in U.S.A.**

Recycling programs for this product may not exist in your area.

**Books by Catherine Mann**

Silhouette Desire

*Baby, I'm Yours* #1721
*Under the Millionaire's Influence* #1787
*The Executive's Surprise Baby* #1837
†*Rich Man's Fake Fiancée* #1878
†*His Expectant Ex* #1895
*Propositioned Into a Foreign Affair* #1941
†*Millionaire in Command* #1969
*Bossman's Baby Scandal* #1988

*Wingmen Warriors
†The Landis Brothers

Silhouette Romantic Suspense

*Wedding at White Sands* #1158
**Grayson's Surrender* #1175
**Taking Cover* #1187
**Under Siege* #1198
*The Cinderella Mission* #1202
**Private Maneuvers* #1226
**Strategic Engagement* #1257
**Joint Forces* #1293
**Explosive Alliance* #1346
**The Captive's Return* #1388
**Awaken to Danger* #1401
**Fully Engaged* #1440
*Holiday Heroes* #1487
  "Christmas at His Command"
**Out of Uniform* #1501

Silhouette Books

**Anything, Anywhere, Anytime*

## CATHERINE MANN

RITA® Award winner Catherine Mann resides on a sunny Florida beach with her military flyboy husband and their four children. Although after nine moves in twenty years, she hasn't given away her winter gear! With over a million books in print in fifteen countries, she has also celebrated five RITA® Award finals, three Maggie Award of Excellence finals and a Booksellers' Best win. A former theater school director and university teacher, she graduated with a master's degree in theater from UNC-Greensboro and a bachelor's degree in fine arts from the College of Charleston. Catherine enjoys hearing from readers and chatting on her message board—thanks to the wonders of the wireless Internet that allow her to cyber-network with her laptop by the water! To learn more about her work, visit her Web site, www.CatherineMann.com, or reach her by snail mail at P.O. Box 6065, Navarre, FL 32566.

I'm truly blessed to work with an AMAZING group of writing industry professionals! Hugs and thanks to the fabulously talented Emilie Rose, Maya Banks, Michelle Celmer, Jennifer Lewis and Leanne Banks. Ladies, it's been a delight and an honor to collaborate with you on this project. Abundant appreciation to my brilliant editor Diana Ventimiglia and my savvy agent Barbara Collins Rosenberg. And my unending gratitude to the whole Harlequin/Silhouette Books team for bringing my books to life!

# Prologue

*New York City, four months ago*

Lauren Presley wondered how a man could be so deeply inside her and yet totally distant at the same time. But no doubt about it, the sated, half-dressed man tangled up with her on her sofa at work had emotionally left the building.

She would boot the rest of him out of her deserted office as soon as she could breathe again.

The butter-soft leather of her turquoise couch stuck to the backs of her legs through her thigh-high stockings, sweat still slicking her body from their frenetically passionate—and surprise—hookup. At least her fledgling graphic-arts business was closed for the day, the workplace empty.

Everything seemed out of sorts, disconnected like a Salvador Dali painting. She couldn't blame Jason for regretting their impulsive act, since she was pretty much freaking out, too, over how fast her panties had landed on the floor, her dress up around her waist while she'd torn at his belt buckle and zipper. Jason Reagert was a business colleague, one half of a working alliance they may very well have wrecked. She needed to get through this awkward post-sex moment ASAP with her pride intact.

A low drone filled the quiet of the empty office. Lauren tensed. "Your pants are vibrating."

Jason arched back and raised a dark eyebrow, his close-cropped hair mussed on top from her fingers. "Pardon?"

She clapped her hand on his warm hip—beside his BlackBerry. "Seriously. It's buzzing."

"Damn." He disentangled himself, cool air brushing her bared legs. Jason swung his feet to the floor, his Testoni loafers thunking against the scarred wood as he sat and unclipped the handheld. "Helluva bad timing."

Avoiding his eyes, she slid upright and adjusted her silky black wrap dress, putting it in place again. Her panties would have to wait. She kicked the scrap of ebony satin under the sofa. "Your pillow talk leaves something to be desired."

"Sorry." His zipper closing rasped, overloud in the late-night silence. "It's my reminder alarm."

"Alarm for what?" She stared nervously at the white brick walls, the easel in the corner, the artwork on lit screens.

"My flight to California."

Right.

He was leaving.

Lauren stood, smoothing her dress and looking for her favorite Manolo leopard pumps that she wouldn't be able to wear again without thinking of this stupid, impetuous night.

She and Jason had been wrapping up final details on a graphic-art design project she'd freelanced for his last ad campaign at the New York firm—he was leaving his NYC job and heading to greener career pastures in California. The job at Maddox Communications in San Francisco was a great opportunity for him. She'd known about this for a couple of weeks. And as she'd hugged him goodbye tonight, she'd been knocked off balance by how upset she was over his impending move.

One second she'd been looking up at his leanly handsome face while blinking back tears, and the next second they'd been kissing... and more. Pleasure prickled down her spine, settling low, as she remembered the bold sweep of his tongue and his hands, his strength as he'd cupped her bottom and lifted her against him. Already her body ached to reach for him again, grab hold of that tie she'd never quite managed to undo and tug him toward her. The impulse was too much, too strong.

Too overwhelming.

Gathering her shredded self-control, she looked away from his strong cheekbones and tempting mouth. She didn't know where all these frenetic feelings had come from and wasn't sure how to undo them now that he was leaving.

She spied her leopard-print shoes under the desk and welcomed the chance to put some space between herself and Jason and a sofa that smelled of good sex. She knelt, pulling one pump free, but the other stayed annoyingly out of reach.

"Lauren—" his loafer-clad feet stopped beside her, making her all the more aware of her ungainly butt-up position "—I don't make a habit of—"

"Stop." She sat back on her feet, willing away one of those awful blushes that came with her auburn-head complexion. "You don't need to say anything." Echoes of her mother's humiliating pleas for her husband to stay bounced around in Lauren's head.

"I'll call—"

"No!" Standing, she gave up on her shoes, her toes curling against the cool wood floor. "Don't make promises you aren't certain you'll keep."

He scooped his suit jacket from the back of a contoured metal chair. "*You* could call *me*."

"What would that accomplish?" She faced him full on for the first time, taking in his prep-school good looks, hardened with an edge from his years in the Navy. He came from old money and had made his fair share of new, as well. "You're moving to California, and New York City is my home. It's not like we have any kind of real connection beyond being work acquaintances who happened to get caught up in a fluky hormonal maelstrom. Nothing to disrupt our entire lives over."

Shaking her long, loose hair back, she opened the door to the larger studio outside, empty but for vacant rolling chairs pushed haphazardly up to tables.

He braced a hand on the door frame, his arrogant brown eyes revealing a hint of surprise. "You're giving me the brush-off?"

Apparently Jason Reagert wasn't told no often. Of

course she'd been mighty quick to say yes, something she intended to change starting now.

"I'm simply being realistic, Jason." She stared him down, her spine straight in spite of the fact he stood at least a head taller.

Later, away from him, she would hole up in her cute little one-bedroom apartment in the Upper East Side. Or better yet, hide out in the Metropolitan Museum of Art for the entire day, crawling into the world of each painting. Her art was everything. She couldn't forget that. This business—bought with a surprise inheritance from her dear elderly aunt Eliza—was her big chance to make her dreams come true. To prove to her mother she was worth something more than a debutante slot and lucrative marriage.

She refused to let any man derail her.

Finally Jason nodded. "Okay, that's the way you want it, that's the way things will be." He skimmed back her hair with his knuckles, his callused thumb stroking her cheekbone. "Goodbye, Lauren."

She settled her features into a portrait worthy of any Dutch master—solemn and unrelenting. Jason turned away, his jacket hooked on one finger over his shoulder, and she fought back the urge to call out to him.

Hearing he was leaving New York had brought a surprise pinch of regret. But nothing compared to the twist in her gut as she watched him walk out the door.

# One

*San Francisco, Present Day*

Working Lauren Presley out of his system had turned out to be tougher than Jason Reagert thought when he'd left New York. But up until sixty seconds ago, he'd been giving it a damn good try.

Clinking glasses, frenetic conversation and blaring eighties music in the high-end bar swelled more tightly around him. He looked up from the photo on his Black-Berry to the woman he'd been flirting with for the past half hour, then back down at the just-in image of Lauren Presley celebrating New Year's Day.

An unmistakably *pregnant* Lauren Presley.

He wasn't often at a loss for words—he was considered a major player in the advertising business, after all.

But right now? His mind blanked. Maybe because his brain was suddenly filled with visions of that impulsive encounter in her office. Had that surprise—mind-blowing—night produced a baby? He hadn't spoken to Lauren since then, but she hadn't called, either. Certainly not with any pregnancy news. He blinked twice fast, the bar coming into focus again.

Pink mirrored walls cast a rosy glow as he studied the shocker image just sent by an NYC pal. He schooled his face to remain neutral while he figured out the best way to make contact with Lauren. She'd sure shown him the door fast enough the last time they'd seen each other.

Some guy gyrating to overloud music jostled him from behind and Jason angled to shield the BlackBerry screen from the packed clientele at the local martini bar on Stockton Street. Rosa Lounge was small and quaint and very expensive, pretty dim on the inside but still classy, with green glass tables and black-lacquered chairs.

A white marble bar took up the majority of one wall with bottles suspended overhead, while tall tables lined the other wall, dark wood floors stretching between. Since Rosa Lounge was just a block away from Maddox Communications, right on the park, MC employees tended to gather here when they closed a big deal or finished a major presentation.

His grip tightened on the BlackBerry. This gathering had been called in honor of him. What rotten timing to be the center of attention.

"Hello?" Celia Taylor snapped her manicured fingers in front of his face twice, her Key Lime Martini sparkling through the crystal glass in her other hand. "Hello? Earth to Jason."

He forced his thoughts and focus to Celia, another ad agent at Maddox Communications. Thank God he hadn't even started drinking his Sapporo. He didn't need the top-shelf brew messing with his head. "Right. I'm here. Sorry to zone out on you like that." He tucked the BlackBerry into his suit jacket. The stored photo damn near seared through his Armani jacket and shirt. "Can I get you a refill?"

He'd been about to offer her more—a date—but then the photo had buzzed through. Technology sure did have an ironic sense of timing.

"I'm good." Celia tapped her painted nail against her martini glass. "That must be one hefty work e-mail. I could get insulted by the fact I'm not warranting your full attention, except I'm just jealous my cell phone isn't buzzing."

Celia flicked her bright red hair over her shoulder and perched a hand on her slender hip.

Red hair.

Green eyes.

Like Lauren. Damn. Realization kicked him in the conscience.

He'd deluded himself into thinking he was putting Lauren behind him this evening, only to try to pick up the lone redhead in the room. Of course, Lauren had darker, auburn hair and softer curves that had driven him crazy exploring....

Jason set his bottle on the bar and eyed the door, mind made up. Delaying wasn't an option. He had to know. But he also didn't want to alienate Celia.

She was a genuinely nice woman who tried to put on a tough facade in order to be taken seriously in the workplace. She deserved better than to be seen as a substitute for another woman. "Sorry to cut out, but I really need to return a call."

Celia cocked her head to the side, her nose scrunched in confusion before she shrugged. "Sure, whatever. Catch you later." She fanned a wave and pivoted on her spiky heel toward fellow ad exec Gavin.

Jason shouldered sideways through the crush of people in power suits, looking for the best way to duck out so he could place a few phone calls. And find answers.

A hand slid from the press of bodies and clapped him on the shoulder. He turned to find both Maddox brothers, the heads of Maddox Communications—CEO Brock and VP Flynn.

Flynn waved other MC employees nearby to join in and then lifted his drink in toast. "To the man of the hour, Jason Reagert! Congratulations on landing the Prentice account. You've done Madd Comm proud."

"To the wonderboy," CFO Asher Williams called.

"Reagert rules," Gavin cheered.

"Unstoppable," Brock declared, his executive assistant echoing the toast.

Jason pulled a smile for appearances. Bringing in the Prentice Group was undoubtedly a coup, although timing had certainly come into play in winning over the country's largest clothing manufacturing company. Landing Prentice was the next best thing to nabbing Procter & Gamble. Jason had only just moved to California in the fall when Walter Prentice dumped his other PR firm for moral-clause violations.

The ultraconservative Prentice had a rep for ditching firms for anything from hearing that the account exec had visited a local nude beach to realizing an exec was dating two women at once. Jason's eyes flicked to Celia.

Brock dipped a wedge of pork quesadilla in mango sauce. The workaholic had most likely missed lunch. "Spoke with Prentice today and he made a point of singing your praises. Good move sharing those war stories with him."

Jason's feet itched to get to the door. And damn it, he hadn't shared the war stories as a schmooze move. He'd simply discovered a connection there since Prentice's nephew had done a tour about the same time as he had. "Only making polite conversation with the client."

Flynn lifted his glass again. "You're a hero, man. The way you and that SEAL team took out those pirates back in the day…epic."

He'd served his six years in the Navy after college graduation. He'd been a dive officer with a specialty in explosive ordinance disposal, attached to a SEAL team. Sure, he'd helped take out some pirates, saved a few lives, but so had the others around him. "I was only doing my job, same as anyone else."

Brock finished off his dinner with a final bite. "You're definitely on Prentice's radar. Keep your nose clean and you'll go far with his influence. Landing Prentice's clothing line couldn't be better timed, especially with Golden Gate Promotions breathing down our necks."

Golden Gate was their main rival, another family-owned advertising agency with quite a pedigree and still helmed by its original founder, Athos Koteas. Jason understood well the specter that rival cast. This job at Maddox—this chance in California—was everything to him. He wouldn't let anything screw it up.

His BlackBerry buzzed again from inside his jacket. More pictures? Was the guy sending him an ultrasound photo, for crying out loud? His gut pitched. He liked kids, sure, wanted some of his own.

Someday.

Flynn ducked in closer. "We consider it quite a coup, you charging in with a winning pitch after that lame ass was fired."

Brock smiled sardonically. "Lame ass? Sunburned ass maybe, after hanging out on that beach au naturel."

Low laughter rumbled up from the clustered bunch of MC employees. Jason slid his finger along the neck of his shirt. What a time to remember that Walter Prentice had reportedly disowned his own granddaughter for refusing to marry the father of her kid. Prentice lived by his motto Family Is Everything.

Performance on the job should be all that mattered, damn it. He'd already been dubbed the golden boy at Maddox Communications, a title he'd worked hard to achieve and would do anything to keep. The key word? *Worked.* He'd earned his way to the top, determined to shed the trust-fund label that had dogged him growing up. He wouldn't allow an impulsive move from four months ago to wreck his chances for the success he'd damn well paid for.

He'd walked away from the carrot of joining his old man's advertising company and took a Navy ROTC scholarship to college instead. After serving his six years, he'd launched out on his own in the ad world. While he'd tackled the New York City job, he could still feel his father's influence breathing down his neck. The offer from San Francisco–based MC had put a whole country between him and the old man's far-reaching shadow.

And just that fast, inspiration hit.

As soon as he finished up here at Rosa Lounge, Jason would be on the red-eye to New York. By morning, he would be on Lauren Presley's doorstep for a face-to-face with her. If that baby was his, she would simply have to come to California.

Any possible rumors would be taken care of when he introduced her as his fiancée.

The icy January wind kept most people indoors. Normally Lauren would have been in her apartment in warm wooly socks, tending her plants. But the cold helped calm her nausea. So she worked on the roof, checking the winterizing on the community garden she'd started a couple of years ago.

Kneeling, she tucked the plastic tighter along the edges of the rooftop planter while roaring engines and horns announced that the Big Apple was waking up. The city in winter wore the neutral palette of an Andrew Wyeth painting, a world reduced to blacks and whites, grays and browns. Icy-cold concrete stung through her jeans as she knelt, a bitter breeze whipping off the East River. She huddled deeper into her wool coat. She flexed her numbed fingers inside her gardening gloves.

Her stomach fluttered from more than the baby.

She'd gotten a panicked call from her friend Stephanie informing her that her husband had let Jason know about the pregnancy via a photo taken at last week's New Year's party.

And now Jason was on his way to NYC.

No amount of cold air or gardening would stem the tide of nausea this time. Her world was totally falling apart. Jason was on his way to confront her about the baby she hadn't gotten around to informing him was due in five months, and oh, by the way, her business was all but in ruins.

Lauren sagged back against the concrete fountain, water frozen in the base, icicles dripping from the stone lion's mane. A week ago she'd learned her bookkeeper, Dave, had used her sick leave as an opportunity to embezzle half a million dollars from her fledgling graphic-design business. She'd only found out when she hired a temp bookkeeper to take over while Dave went "on vacation." Now they all knew he wouldn't be returning from whatever island haven he'd taken up residence at using her money. Authorities didn't hold out much hope of finding him—or her funds.

She rubbed a hand over the growing curve of her belly. A child completely dependent on her and she'd royally screwed up her life. What kind of mother would she make? A total coward, up here hiding.

Things had changed so much in a few months. She missed the color palette of spring and summer, but her artistic eye still appreciated the monochromatic starkness of a winter landscape.

The rooftop door creaked a second before a long shadow stretched over her. She knew before she looked. Jason had found her anyway. There was no more delaying this confrontation.

Lauren glanced over her shoulder and... She felt a shiver of awareness.

Jason's lean, looming presence added the final touch

to the stark skyline, his swimmer's build, dark hair cut short, thicker along the top and just lifting in the harsh wind. He stood tall, immovable, uncompromising—physically and emotionally.

She turned away and tucked her gardening tools back in her bag. "Hello, Jason."

His footsteps grew louder, closer, and still he didn't speak.

"I guess the doorman told you I was up here," she babbled, her hands frantically busy.

He knelt beside her. "You should be more careful."

She inched away. "You shouldn't sneak up on people."

"What if it hadn't been me coming up here? That door creaks mighty damn loud and you were in another world."

"Okay, you're right. I was, uh, distracted." By his impending arrival, the baby on the way, and oh, yeah, she had an embezzler on her payroll. So much for her insistence she was ready to take on the world.

She could almost hear her parents' disapproval about everything in her life. Except for Jason. He was exactly the sort of man her socialite mother would pick for her, with his blue-blood lineage, fat bank account and good looks.

Hell, most any mom would be happy to have Jason Reagert as a son-in-law. But he was also stubborn and controlling and she'd fought too hard for her independence to risk it in a relationship with this man. No doubt that was why she'd succeeded in ignoring the attraction for the past months.

She clutched her bag to her chest. "What are you doing here? You could have just called."

"And *you* could have called." He looked at her

stomach and back up again. "When I spoke with a friend of mine back here last night, he told me you've been working from home because you're not feeling well. Are you all right? Is the baby all right?"

And there it was. Her pregnancy news out there with a simple statement. No huge confrontation or shouting match like her parents would have had before—and after—their divorce. All the same, her fingers shook, so she hitched her bag over her shoulder and stood.

"Only morning sickness." She stuffed her hands in her pockets. "The doctor says I'm fine. I'm just more productive if I work from home. The worst is past."

"I'm glad to hear that."

The nausea had been debilitating for a couple of months. Entrusting so much of the office routine to others had been nerve-racking, but there hadn't been any other choice. Too bad it had cost her so much. "I made it back up to half days in the office last week."

"Are you sure you're ready? You look like you've lost weight." A protective gleam lit his eyes. He grabbed an iron chair and hauled it over to her.

Lauren glanced at him warily before sitting. "How much do you know about the pregnancy?"

"Does it matter?" He shrugged out of his trench coat and draped it over her shoulders.

The familiar scent of his aftershave mingled with his body warmth clinging to the fabric. Too tempting. She passed his coat back because she couldn't handle even one more obstacle in her life. Not now. "I guess not, as long as you do know."

He stepped closer, his dark eyes intense in a way that

sent shivers up her spine and had even led her to ditch her panties four months ago.

She forced herself to look away, reminded too thoroughly of the feelings that had propelled her into his arms the first time. "Thank you for believing me."

"I would say thanks for telling me, but you didn't." The first hint of anger tinted his tones.

"I would have, eventually." Before the kid graduated from college, at this rate. "The baby isn't due for five more months."

"I want to be a part of my child's life, every moment. Starting now, we'll work together."

"You're moving back to New York?"

"No." He flipped the collar on his trench coat up over his ears, his suntanned face declaring how much he'd already acclimated to the more temperate California weather. "Let's take this conversation to your apartment where there's heat."

Then a sneaking suspicion seeped in deeper than the damp cold. "You're not moving back to New York, but you want us to work together bringing up the baby. You can't actually expect me to move to San Francisco, can you?"

His silence confirmed her suspicion.

Her anger rose. "I'm not going anywhere with you. Not to my apartment and not to California. You really expect me to uproot my life? To abandon the company I've put my heart and soul into?" If there was even a company left to look after.

"Fine—" the word burst from his mouth in a gust of cloudy cold white "—yes, I want you to come to San Francisco. I want us to be together for our baby. What's more important—your company or your child?"

She wanted to shout that she had put her child's welfare first at the cost of her business. And she knew she would do the same all over again. She only wished she'd shelled out extra dollars for someone more reliable to watch over the shop, instead of worrying about her tight budget and blindly trusting the people she'd hired to do their damn jobs.

"Jason, why are you being so pushy so fast?" Some—okay, a lot—of her anger and fear from work directed itself at Jason. "There's time for us to talk through this, months, in fact. What's really going on here?"

His face closed up, all frustration hidden until he looked as cold as the frozen lion fountain. "I don't know what you mean."

"There must be a reason for the sudden hard sell to put me in the same state as you." Wind whistled louder, almost drowning out the sounds of street traffic below. "Was your mother abandoned by some scum bucket of a man? Did a woman do you wrong in the past?"

His laughter burst out in a fresh gust of puffy clouds until he shook his head. "You have an active imagination. I can assure you that I have none of those tortured scenarios in my past."

His laughter was infectious—and distracting. "That's not a complete answer."

"I'm not here to fight with you." He stepped closer, the ocean-fresh scent of him teasing her pregnancy-heightened senses.

Warmth radiated off him in a welcome wave and contrast to the bitter cold. She ached to burrow against his chest and feel the lean coil of his muscles rippling against her. Tension gathered low and hot and fast as it always had around him, but even more so now that she knew how explosive they could be together.

She raised her hands between them, stopping just shy of actually touching his chest. Wary of even touching him to nudge him away. "You're moving too fast for me. I need time to think."

"Well, while you're thinking, keep this in mind." He slid a hand into his pocket and pulled out a black velvet ring box. He creaked open the lid to reveal…

A platinum-set solitaire diamond engagement ring.

# Two

Jason held the velvet box in his hand and waited for Lauren's answer. Getting a jeweler to open up after hours had been a challenge, but he'd managed in time to catch the red-eye flight.

The shock on Lauren's face wasn't a great sign, but he was used to overcoming difficult odds. Wind stirred dry leaves around their feet, so frigidly different from the summer evening they'd spent working after hours in her office.

He extended his hand with the engagement ring, knowing he was being impatient, but time was short. "So? What's the verdict?"

"Whoa, hold on." She gathered her long straight hair back from her face and exhaled—hard. "I'm still stuck back on your idea that I would uproot myself to come to California and now you're tossing an engagement into the mix?"

"Does this look like I'm joking?" He lifted the diamond. The morning sun refracted off all three carats.

The gardening bag slid from her shoulder and thudded to the ground. "You really expect us to get married just because I'm pregnant? That's archaic."

He hadn't meant marriage. He'd been thinking more along the lines of an engagement to shut up any gossips, something she might appreciate, too. But telling her as much probably wouldn't go over well. "If agreeing to marriage moves too fast for you, I'll settle for a trial engagement."

"Trial engagement? You're out of your freaking mind and I'm freezing." She turned toward the door. "You're right about one thing. We should move this conversation to my apartment."

He picked up the canvas bag she'd left on the ground—the only sign she might be nervous—and followed her down two flights of stairs to the third floor. Her place was safe by New York standards, but somehow that didn't seem like enough now. And where would an active toddler play?

He'd had a lot of time to think on that flight, and one thing he'd settled on for certain—he didn't want to be a bicoastal dad. He wanted to be a larger part of his child's life. Sure, he worked hard, but he wasn't going to be like his father, who'd expected Jason to be a carbon copy of him, while never spending any time with his son to actually get to know him.

He needed to lure Lauren to California for more reasons than the Prentice account. He tucked the ring back in his pocket—for now. His goal set, he waited while she unlocked the double bolts and swept the door wide.

Her one-bedroom apartment reflected her personality. Vibrant. Alive. Packed with flowers, plants and colorful framed fabrics, an oasis in the middle of winter. Each area was painted a different color—the living room yellow, the kitchen green.

A hint of pink showed past her partly open bedroom door. He'd joined others from work for drinks at her apartment before, out here in the living area, but he'd never seen the bedroom up close. Something he intended to change down the road.

He set her bag on the hall table and followed her inside, wiping his feet on a rag rug. "We were friends for months, and we're obviously attracted to each other." He gestured toward her stomach. "Can you honestly say you never considered a future between us?"

"Never." She hung her coat on one of the vintage doorknobs mounted on a strip of wood, glancing back over her shoulder at him. "Now could you wrap this up, please? We can talk later about logistics for after the baby is born, but right now, I need to get ready for work."

"Wow, no worries of a guy getting an inflated ego around you." This didn't seem to be a wise time to bring up how fast she'd kicked him out of her office four months ago. Besides, she looked tired. Fine lines of exhaustion furrowed her forehead. His instincts went on alert. "Are you sure you're all right?"

She hesitated a second too long before walking away toward the green galley kitchen. "I'm fine."

He tracked her movements as she poured a glass of milk, her silky red hair swinging along her back and inviting his hands to test the texture, to discover if it was as soft as he remembered. "There's something you're not telling me."

"I promise the baby and I are both totally healthy." She lifted her glass in toast, her back still toward him.

She was dodging something, he was sure, but he could also sense she wouldn't share more now. He would be best served by a temporary retreat before advancing his cause again in a few hours.

He was an ad guy, after all. He knew how to make a pitch, and for now, he needed to back off. The right opportunity would present itself.

Jason pulled the box out of his pocket and set it on the small butcher-block counter. "Just hang on to this for now. We don't have to decide anything today."

She eyed the box as if it contained a snake. "I already know there's no way in hell we're getting engaged, much less married."

"Fair enough." He nudged the box forward until it rested beside an apple-shaped ceramic cookie jar. "Save the ring for our kid."

Turning toward him, she sagged back against the counter, her T-shirt with paint splatters hugging her pregnant belly—and her fuller breasts. "You seem sure it's a girl."

His eyes dropped back to her stomach, his own gut clenching tight as an image of a little girl with red curls filled his head. This baby was real and growing inside Lauren just an arm's reach away. He'd barely had time to process the idea of being a father, much less see the proof so visibly. His hands itched to touch Lauren, to explore the differences in her.

To feel the baby kick?

His throat went tight. "It could be a boy, who'll one day need an engagement ring to give some girl."

She tipped her head to the side, her silky hair gliding over the rounded curves of her breasts. "Do you want a boy? Seems that most men prefer to have a son first."

"Is that how things were with your dad?" His own father sure as hell had wanted a mini-version of himself, someone to mirror his every move, decision, thought.

Her face closed up. "This isn't about my father."

"Okay, then." He gave in to temptation and stroked back a lock of her hair, sliding his hand away before she could protest. "You look beautiful but tired, and I seem to recall you saying something about needing to go to work." He dropped a kiss on her forehead, resisting the urge to linger and, instead, making a beeline for the door. "Goodbye, Lauren. We'll talk later."

He stepped into the hall, her confused face stamped on his memory, fueling him in his decision to retreat for the moment, keep her off balance. She had doubts and he could play on those.

She may have said no this morning, but he wasn't down for the count. Without question, by the time he took the last flight out on Sunday night, Lauren would be coming to California with his child.

Lauren pushed through the glass door leading into the fourth-floor offices that housed her graphic-design business. Not much space, actually, just a common room with tables, a receptionist desk by the door and her own office in back. Where she and Jason had made this baby.

At the moment she couldn't blame the pregnancy for her churning stomach. Her insides swirled around like a Jackson Pollock color extravaganza.

The small velvet ring box seemed to weigh ten tons in her purse—a sack of a bag made from an old sweater she'd found at a consignment store. She'd packed up the jewelry so she could call Jason, schedule a lunch and return the ring. An engagement was a ludicrous idea.

She had enough on her plate, anyhow, finding a way to save her business from bankruptcy.

Franco, her secretary, passed her a stack of memo sheets. "Ms. Presley, your messages."

"Thanks, Franco." She forced herself to smile.

Lauren shuffled through the inch-thick pile; calls from prospective clients were mixed in with phone numbers from creditors.

Franco stood, smoothing down his NY Giants tie. "Before you go into your office—"

"Yes," she answered, opening her door at the same time. The floral scent wafted out.

Franco shrugged and leaned back. "They were delivered just before you arrived. And, uh..."

His voice dwindled off in her mind as she turned to find her office packed with at least five vases of white rosebuds with pink and blue ribbons. On the corner of her desk, she saw a carafe of juice and basket of muffins. She spun back to hear what else Franco was saying.

Movement drew her attention to the far recesses of the reception area, where Jason lounged, assessing her with sexy, hooded eyes. How had she missed him when she came in? And why hadn't Franco told...? Okay, so Franco had tried.

Lauren nodded Jason into her office. "Come on. You might as well eat with me."

He shoved away from the wall, slowly, lean and lanky, like a predator cougar as he strode toward her. Franco, the new accountant and the two interns from NYU looked from Jason to her with undisguised curiosity.

Jason slid his arm around her waist. "I wanted to make sure the mother of my child is well fed and happy."

She stiffened under his touch. Damn his presumptuous ass. Just that fast he'd announced their relationship to the world. Well, not the world, but to her employees and three waiting clients.

"The baby and I are fine, thank you." She planted a hand in the middle of his back and pushed. "Can I speak with you in my office, please?"

"Of course, dear," he said with smooth affection and a charming smile that had the two interns giggling and blushing.

She closed her office door, sealing her in the room with Jason. Alone. With the turquoise sofa. With a host of memories.

Lauren opened the white metal blinds and let the sun blast through. Not that it did much to defuse her anger. "What the hell was that all about?"

"Only letting people know I care about you and our child." He picked up a fat blueberry muffin. "Breakfast?"

"I've already eaten. Don't you think you should have checked to see if I'd told the folks at work about the baby?"

He paused. "You've told them. You've been on sick leave."

"Fine, you're right. But the clients in the waiting area didn't know, and this is my announcement to make to the world when I'm darn well ready."

"You're right, and I'm sorry." He waved the muffin closer, near enough for her to catch a whiff. "Now would you like something to eat? The bakery made them fresh this morning. I saw them come out of the oven."

She wanted to tell the pushy man what he could do with his muffins. But damned if she wasn't starving all over again as she looked at those plump blueberries straining at the sides, the sweet crumble topping making her lick her lips in anticipation. While she loved her baby, sometimes she really resented these hormones that seemed to have such Herculean control over her body.

That same hormonal storm was making her go all teary-eyed over the flowers and food because, God, this was what first-time parents did for each other. The past few months had been so damn hard without the support of a partner. She didn't even want to think about how difficult the coming months—years—might be.

For now she just wanted to enjoy her muffin.

Her feet carried her closer, until she stood toe to toe with Jason. Sniffing back her tears, she could smell him and the flowers and the muffin, and, gracious, but all of it smelled mouthwateringly good. Jason pinched off a piece and brought it to her lips. She parted for him before she could think, pretty damn much the way she'd done on that sofa four months ago.

What was it about this man that made her act so out of character? She wasn't wildly impulsive like her erratic mother. She had control over her emotions. Except for a most memorable lapse around Jason.

She took the bready bite and her senses exploded with pleasure over the sweet fruit melting on her tongue. Jason's thumb traced along her bottom lip, stroking, stirring a whirlpool of want inside her until her breasts tightened in response beneath her brown wool sweaterdress. She arched up on her toes inside her burnt-orange pumps, a whisper away from his mouth—

A knock rattled her office door.

"What?" Her voice came out breathy and impatient. She didn't move. Neither did Jason, the heat of his brown eyes sizzling through her.

The knocking continued, more insistent now. Lauren cleared her throat and tried again. "Yes?" she said, stepping back, not a hundred percent sure who that "yes" was for. "What do you need?"

Jason smiled, wicked and sexy as if to say exactly what he needed. Here. Now.

Lauren clasped the doorknob, willing her professional composure back into place. "What can I help you with?"

She found the grandmotherly accountant she'd hired to sort through the financial mess. The brisk woman waited, hand raised for another knock. Talk about a splash of ice-water reality to douse her passion! She needed to tend to this now, but didn't need Jason to hear.

Lauren said, her voice low, "I'll be with you in five minutes."

The accountant tucked the files against her chest. Her keen eyes proclaimed loud and clear that no one would steal cookies from the jar on her watch. "Good, good. We can go over the preliminary financial statement, with a list of the most pressing creditors."

"Of course." She glanced at Jason, nerves gnawing.

She needed him gone. "Jason, we'll have to talk later. Tonight, after work."

He frowned. "Creditors?"

"It's not your problem," she said, dodging his question.

His chest expanded in a manner she'd come to recognize as territorial. "You're the mother of my child. If something pertains to you, it's my problem too."

She angled toward the accountant. "I'll meet you in your office in five minutes."

Lauren closed the door and leaned back against it, facing Jason. The genuine concern in his eyes caught her off guard. She was so on the defensive these days, she'd all but forgotten what a champion he could be. In their year as friends, more than once she'd seen him go to the mat for someone else—a guy fired unjustly, a woman with a stalker boyfriend, even taking on the account of a company pro bono when he'd learned the owner's kid had inordinately high medical bills.

Jason Reagert was pushy, but a goodhearted kind of pushy. It wasn't surprising he'd found his way to military service for so many years.

She could cut him some slack while still keeping her boundaries in place. "It will be public knowledge soon enough when charges are filed, so you might as well know. My accountant, the one before this new lady, embezzled half a million dollars from my company."

His eyebrows shot up toward his dark hairline. "When did this happen?"

"While I was working from home." She pushed away from the door and sagged to sit on the sofa, suddenly weary all over again. If she couldn't tell the guy who'd knocked her up, who could she tell? "I had some suspicions about Dave just before I got sick and planned on firing him. Then I spent a week in the hospital for dehydration. I was relieved when he turned in his resignation. I gave him two weeks' paid vacation and had him escorted out of the office. Three days later I hired a new accountant, the one I should have hired in the first place, but I was trying to save money." She shrugged. "I guess it's true that you get what you pay for."

He sat beside her, not touching, not crowding her for once since he'd shown up on her roof. "I'm so damn sorry."

"Me, too."

"No wonder you were upset this morning." He clasped his hands loosely between his knees, his Rolex glinting in the light shining through the open blinds. "You don't need this kind of worry, especially when you're pregnant. Let me help."

So much for not crowding her. "Whoa, back up. I may be in trouble, but I'll handle it."

"There's nothing wrong with accepting help." He stretched his arm along the sofa back, wrapping her in his scent if not his arms. "In fact, that's why I'm here. I need *your* help."

"With what?" she asked warily, wondering if she was talking with the altruistic Jason, who went to the mat for people.

Or the shark of an ad man who won accounts through his unerring ability to make people believe anything he said.

"I'm new at Maddox Communications and times are tight. No job is secure." His chocolate-brown eyes seemed sincere, intense.

"I can understand that."

"I'm not sure how much you know about MC...."

"It's a family-owned business." She hadn't worked with Maddox before, but the grapevine said they'd hooked some hefty clients. "Run by two brothers, right?"

"Right, Brock Maddox is the CEO and Flynn is the vice president. The one thing standing in the way of the company's domination out West is Golden Gate Promotions."

"That's a family-owned advertising business, too, isn't it?" She relaxed into the sofa, more comfortable in their familiar ground of talking shop. "Athos Koteas still runs the show. I haven't worked with him, but I've heard he's quite a force to be reckoned with. Absolutely ruthless."

"But successful." His arm on the back of the sofa radiated a warmth that made the roots of her hair tingle. "He's a Greek immigrant who made quite a splash, which brought in many European connections to give his company a leg up in these tough last few years. Now he's trying to encroach on Maddox's clients." His face went tight with irritation. "He's put some rumors out there to make Maddox Communications seem untrustworthy and now they're losing business. It's causing Brock even more headaches."

"Are you regretting the move to California?"

"Not at all. Things are going better at work. I've brought in some new clients, one big fish in particular. But that client is extremely conservative. You may have heard of him—Walter Prentice."

Holy crap. "Congratulations, Jason. That's amazing. Landing Prentice isn't just reeling in a big fish. The Prentice account is a freaking whale."

"A whale with the motto Family Is Everything.

Prentice fired his last ad guy for going to a nude beach." Shaking his head, Jason pulled his arm back. "He disowned his only granddaughter for not marrying the father of her baby."

Wait, he couldn't really be suggesting... "You can't expect me to believe they'll fire you because you have a pregnant ex-girlfriend." Okay, so she'd never been his girlfriend. But still. She flopped back on the sofa. "Give me a break."

He held up both hands. "I'm serious as a heart attack. The guy's offering up a seven-figure ad campaign in tough economic times. He gets to call the shots and choose whoever he wants."

She eyed her bag with the ring inside—a ring that hadn't been romantic at all. It hadn't even been offered out of old-fashioned chivalry. He wanted to keep his job.

A cold core grew heavy in the middle of her chest. "You're that ambitious."

"Aren't you?" He leaned closer, eyes intent. "You and I are like-minded. We both want to prove to our families we can make it without their help. So let's work together for the good of our kid."

"Leave my parents out of this!" she snapped before she could think, but her heart hurt when it totally shouldn't have. She knew better than to expect anything from Jason. There had never been talk of feelings between them.

In fact, she preferred her life be less emotional. Less like her mother.

"Fine," he conceded, "it's not about our parents. We'll make this about securing our baby's future by securing our own. I need you to agree to a temporary engagement, just until I've finished with the Prentice account. I'll give you the money you need to tide over your business until you regain your footing."

He was starting to make sense and that scared her. She shoved to her feet, pacing, restless. "I don't need your money. I just need time."

"You can call it a loan if it makes you feel better. A half million, right?"

She toyed with the strap on her purse, all too aware of the ring inside. His offer of money made it all sound so awful. "Do you know what would really make me feel better?"

"Name it." He walked up behind her, quietly, looming without touching. "It's yours."

She spun to face him. "If you took your almighty money and—"

"Okay, okay, I get the picture. You're not interested in saving your company."

She jammed her arm elbow-deep in her purse and fished out the ring. "I'm not interested in handouts."

He clasped his hands behind his back. "I'm offering you a trade."

She thrust the ring toward him. "How can you be so certain this big-account client will even know the baby is yours? We can just stay silent."

His chest expanded. "There's no way in hell I'm denying my own kid for even a day. I may be ambitious, but there are lines. That one's not negotiable."

She pressed the back of her wrist to her forehead, ring box still in her grip. "This is all too much to absorb at once. I just don't know…"

He clasped her shoulders lightly. "Fine, we'll let that ride for now." He massaged gently, his touch both soothing and stirring. "We have more pressing concerns, anyway, making plans for the baby. I'll pick you up after work."

She struggled not to loll into his caress, his comfort. His help. She'd been so tense and scared her whole body ached from knotted muscles. "Do you think for once you could ask rather than command?"

He smoothed his hands down her arms, plucked the ring box from her and set it on her desk. Then he linked their fingers, the first real connection they'd shared since they'd made love in this office four months ago. "Would you like to go out to dinner after work?"

"To discuss plans for the baby."

He nodded, still holding but not moving closer, not crowding, only tempting.

She should know better. But they did have to talk. She couldn't avoid him forever. "Pick me up at my place at seven."

As she watched him leave her office, she couldn't help but wonder if she'd made a mistake bigger than the rock resting in that ring box.

# Three

Phone tucked under her chin, Lauren hopped on one foot, tugging on her purple boot. "Hi, Mom." She dropped onto the edge of her bed. "What can I do for you?"

"Lauren, dear, I've been calling and calling and you never pick up at work, or home, or on your cell," her mother said, rambling a thousand miles an hour at the other end of the line. Her flat New England accent was more pronounced, a sure sign she was worked up. "I'm beginning to think you're dodging me."

"Would I do that?" She'd spoken with her mom just a couple of days ago. Jacqueline Presley had logged in about thirty-seven messages since then. Lauren had enough trouble dealing with her mother in a manic cycle during a regular day.

These days were far from regular.

"I don't know what you'll do, Lauren, I don't know anything about you lately." Her mother paused. For air? To gather her thoughts? "Have you spoken with your father?"

Ah, hell. She needed to steer clear of that ticking bomb. "No, Mother, I haven't given Dad a single minute more of my time than you've gotten."

"There's no need to be snippy. I don't know why you get so uptight. Sometimes you're just like your father's sister, and she ended up alone. And fat."

Great. Just what she needed to hear, her mother's obsession with her daughter's curves. Lauren had probably been the only ten-year-old on the planet who'd known what the term *Rubenesque* meant.

"Didn't mean to offend you, Mom." Perched on the edge of the mattress, Lauren zipped one boot, then the other, glancing at the clock. Jason would be ringing the doorbell any minute now. She'd barely had time to yank on the black stretch pants and long sweater after her workday had run late. She'd tossed her purse onto her bed and the ring box had tumbled out. "Things are just hectic at work."

"You don't have to grind yourself into the ground trying to prove yourself to me." A chain jingled on the other end of the line as Jacqueline Presley undoubtedly fidgeted with her jewel-studded glasses chain. "I can tell your father to release a portion of your inheritance now. Or you could have simply invested that money from Aunt Eliza and had a nice little nest egg while you pursued real art."

Lauren's chest went tight. A typical stress reaction around her mom, especially when Jacqueline went down this path…

"You could be as good an artist as I was, Lauren, if you just applied yourself."

Lauren twisted her fists into her satiny damask bedspread. The debacle with the accountant would only fuel her mother's arguments. She felt ill. "Mom—"

"I'm going to be in the city next week." Jacqueline plowed ahead. "We can lunch."

Good God, once her mother was on a roll with her list of all the ways Lauren wasn't living her life right, it usually ended with a list of eligible young men she'd met. Men Lauren would just *love*. Men like Jason.

Her mother was going to have a cow when she learned about this pregnancy.

"Mom, it's been great talking to you—" she stood, tugging her sweater over her hips "—but I really have to go."

"You have plans?"

And if she didn't? Her mother would keep talking. Might as well be honest. "I do have a dinner date with a work associate. Not a *date* kind of date." Babbling only made things worse, and worst of all made her fear becoming like her mother.

"Please, dear, do go and pretty yourself up. And remember, pink is not your color. Ta-ta." Her mother hung up.

"Argh!" Lauren thumbed the off button so hard her nail polish chipped. She tossed the phone on the bed, pacing and shaking her hands as if she could somehow flick away the irritation.

The hurt.

After all these years, she should have gotten used to her mother, and actually, this conversation hadn't even really been that bad in the big scheme of things. But she could hear the mania building, knew how close her mother was to the edge. One small nudge would send her flying into a full bipolar swing. Since her mother refused medication and therapy lately, the highs and lows grew more extreme.

Finding out about the baby would be more than a small nudge for Jacqueline Presley. Add the embezzlement, and who knew how her mom would react? One thing was certain, her mother wouldn't handle any of the news calmly.

Passing a potted fern under the window, Lauren snapped off a dry frond. What would it be like to have a mother she could turn to right now? Her hand slid to her stomach. She would do whatever it took to be that kind of support for her child.

Lauren turned the fern stand so the other side of the plant received equal time in the sun. If only she could have a few weeks to regain her footing outside the high drama. If she just had some space to gather her thoughts, plan, put her life on track again…

The ring box in the middle of the mattress drew her eyes like a magnet. Her feet followed, leading her toward the bed.

Jason's offer of a temporary engagement spiraled through her mind. Tempting. Dangerous. Could she risk that much time in California in close quarters with him?

Then again, with her life in New York ready to implode and her own health a bit touchy, could she afford not to?

Jason guided the rental car along the two-lane road leading into a quaint small town about forty minutes out of the city. Lauren sat beside him, her head resting back, that crazy sweater purse of hers cradled in her lap against the gentle curve of her stomach.

Of their baby.

He finally had Lauren alone for a few hours and he needed to make the most of them. He'd dug deep for everything he knew about her, had approached the evening as an account he needed to win.

Yeah, thinking of this analytically was a helluva lot easier for him than contemplating how important it had become to win this point. The more he thought about the crook who'd stolen from her business, the more pissed off he got. She was so damn talented. He'd recognized her extraordinary artistic gifts from their very first meeting.

His fist tightened on the luxury sedan's gearshift. The urge to do more than protect—to take action—fired through him, stronger than anything he could remember since he'd been on assignment in the Navy.

Of course, persuading Lauren would be easier if she was awake. She'd been out like a light before they hit the city limits. If she didn't wake up by the time he reached their destination, he would simply circle the block until she woke up or he needed to refuel the car. As much stress as she'd been under, she undoubtedly needed the sleep. And he could press his point better with a well-rested Lauren.

Vintage streetlamps dotted the roadside, casting dim orbs for a shadowy view of the small stores and shops. Snowflakes skittered in front of the sweeping beams of the headlights, the occasional car swishing past in the other lane.

*Ring, ring.* Her cell phone cut through the silent car with soft wind-chime tones, buried deep in her funky sweater purse. Too deep for him to fish out. Would she simply sleep through it?

She stirred, then jolted awake, her long eyelashes sweeping wide and blinking fast. Lauren grabbed her purse and stuffed her hand inside. She pulled out the cell just as the ringing stopped. She frowned.

He turned down the radio, jazz music fading. "Do you need to take that call?"

She shook her head and stuffed her phone back in her bag. "No, it's fine. I can call back later."

"I understand if you have work commitments."

"It's not work." She fidgeted with the handle on her purse, the strap looking as if it was made from the arms of a sweater. "My mother. She calls. A lot."

From her tone it didn't sound as if she looked forward to those calls, but still, they talked. He hadn't spoken with his parents since his dad disowned him, vowing he'd broken his mother's heart by turning his back on everything they'd done for him. Hell, he didn't want to go there in his mind. Better to focus on Lauren. "What did your family have to say about the baby?"

She pitched her purse on the floor. "I haven't told them yet."

Strange. "She calls but she doesn't visit?"

"We haven't seen each other in a month. I only started showing a couple of weeks ago."

"They're going to hear soon. Hell, I heard clear across country. I'll go with you when you tell them."

A laugh burst free. "Who said you're invited, ego man? Besides, they're divorced."

He eased up on the accelerator as they approached a curve, careful to keep the car well below the speed limit. He had precious cargo on board. "I thought we were going to try and get along for the baby's sake."

"Sorry." She folded her arms under her chest and stared out the window, trees stretching ahead in the historic suburb, full of whitewashed fences and brick colonials. "I'm upset about work and taking it out on you."

He wanted to remind her he could fix that work problem in a flash, but decided not to push his luck. Better to go at this from a different angle. "You can't genuinely expect to keep it a secret that I'm the baby's father, can you? Your parents will find out eventually. If they're going to get upset, maybe it would be best to run a preemptive strike. We tell them as a unified front, catch them off guard, then head out before they have a chance to ask questions."

"That sounds good in theory, but the odds of getting both my parents in the same room together are slim to none. And the second one of them finds out, that person will be on the phone blaming the other." She shook her head, her booted feet crossing and uncrossing restlessly, her purple footwear drawing his eyes, not to mention his interest. "I just don't want to put myself through that if I can possibly avoid it."

He couldn't recall her mentioning much about her parents before. They'd mostly talked about work and nightlife in New York. He'd always been attracted to Lauren, but the timing never seemed right to pursue it. First she was seeing someone else, then he was. Although he couldn't even remember who that other woman was now. "Sounds like your parents have really hurt you since they split up."

"Maybe in the past." Her chin tipped, her green eyes glinting from the dashboard glow. "But I don't let them have that kind of power over me anymore."

"Are you sure?" He glanced at her purse with the cell phone. "Just because they had a contentious relationship doesn't mean we'll play out the same problems."

The glimmer in her eyes turned cooler than the snowflakes picking up pace outside. "And just because you've been inside my body doesn't give you the right to crawl inside my head."

"Fair enough." He liked her spunk most of all. When he thought about it, he liked a lot of things about her. Her smarts, her ambition, even her obsession with packing every square inch of her apartment with plants. Then there was the way her cool exterior lit on fire when he'd least expected it.

"That's it? You're backing off?" She looked over at him, her full lips parting in a pretty O of surprise that invited him to lean across...

He held strong. Better not push his luck. Especially when he had thoughts filling his mind of her wearing nothing but her hair.

"You asked me to back off. I'm listening to you." Very closely. Details were important with so much at stake.

He slowed on the tree-lined road, nearing his destination.

She watched him through narrowed eyes. "I've seen you at work. You never give up, you merely change tack. Remember when you went crazy for the sailboat ink drawing I did and vowed to work it into the cologne campaign even though the client was dead set on a cowboy graphic?"

Okay, so that sailboat was now stamped on male cologne bottles around the world—the original drawing framed in his computer room at home. But all that was beside the point. He focused on the goal.

"This is more important than work. I want you calm and happy." Honest enough, and while he was going for truthfulness... "Hell, and it just so happens that I also want you. You were beautiful before, but now you're absolutely stunning."

"Back down, Romeo," she said, but still smiling, as he guided the car up to a small cabin restaurant. "You've already worked your way into my bed."

"It's been a while." Four months that felt like longer and still he hadn't been able to forget her. Irritation nipped. Damn it, he'd had to force himself to offer to buy another woman a drink. A drink, for Pete's sake. He hadn't even asked her for a date.

Lauren pulled out her cell phone and thumbed the keypad.

Jason reigned in his irritation and focused on Lauren. "Your mother again?"

"No, I'm checking the call history." She pursed her lips. "Hmm...four months and not a single call from you. Doesn't seem like you've been pining for me."

Had she been mad that he hadn't called? He'd considered it, but she'd been fast to show him the door after they had sex. Maybe he'd misread her. As much as he prided himself on gauging people, this time, he wouldn't mind being wrong one damn bit.

Maybe she did want a repeat. God knows, he'd

wanted more of her then, wanted more now. Her flowery scent drifted across the car, her soft curves warm, inviting him to pull off somewhere more secluded and tangle up with her. The pregnancy complicated matters, sure. But maybe sex could simplify them again.

Pure want pounded through his veins. "You made it clear our plans for the future didn't jibe."

"That hasn't changed."

"Everything has changed." He shifted in his seat, the leather creaking as he leaned closer to her.

Her pupils dilated. She swayed nearer. Still he waited, taking his time to breathe in the fresh scent of her, the flowers and greenery she worked with.

He slid an arm along the back of her seat, just cupping her shoulder, absorbing the feel of her, remembering. Her curves fit into the curve of his arm, softer, fuller with the swell of pregnancy between them.

He forced himself to move away. "This baby puts a whole new spin on priorities, and the sooner you accept that, the sooner we can move on to the good stuff."

She flopped back with a frustrated sigh. "You have a one-track mind."

He wasn't going to make the same mistake twice. If there was a chance she wanted to resume the sexual relationship, he wouldn't mess it up again by pushing too fast or walking away too soon. Time to start romancing the mother of his child.

Jason flipped his coat collar up and unlocked the car doors. "Let's put this conversation on hold until after supper. I have a surprise for you."

He was certain the specially chosen restaurant would charm her. He just had to hope his best powers of persuasion would be enough to sway this coolly inscrutable woman.

The stakes were too high to consider a loss.

Where had she lost her self-control?

Lauren gripped the banister of the front steps leading up to her apartment building, a restored brownstone. The dinner with Jason had been amazing. His choice of a family-owned Italian restaurant full of plants charmed her. The rustic old homestead was like a warm vineyard inside. Having him notice her love of greenery touched her. He was trying.

She climbed the steps, aware of him at her back. Of course he was trying. He wanted to get his way. Jason Reagert was a driven, ambitious man. Everyone in the ad business knew nothing could stop him when he set his mind to do something. She'd found it admirable when they were work friends.

But as the target of his campaign? She wasn't so sure anymore. What would have been an enjoyable, intimate evening bothered her somehow, made her want the real thing.

No. She wasn't ready to go that far. The ring would stay in her purse a while longer.

She glanced over her shoulder as a car slushed past. "Thank you for the thoughtful dinner. You actually managed to take my mind off the mess at work for a couple of hours."

He turned up his coat collar, his dark hair shiny in the glow of the outdoor lights. "You need to eat. Glad I could be of service."

Lauren twisted her key in the lock. "You're not going

to use my comment as an excuse to press your plan for a fake engagement?"

"You know where I stand. What more is there to say?" He followed her into the building's hallway, apparently in no hurry to call it a night. "And before you ditch me on the stoop, I am going to see you safely to your apartment door."

"For safety's sake?" She gestured around the entryway, soaring ceiling echoing the low voices of a couple down the corridor and the older lady in 2A calling to her poodle for a walk. Nobody would get mugged here. Too many witnesses.

"Somebody's gotta protect you from that vicious pup." He smiled, his five-o'clock shadow adding a bad-boy air to go along with the glint in his eye.

She rolled her eyes and started up the stairs, trying not to think about how long those three flights would feel once she was in her third trimester. "Come on, then."

He followed, a wooden stair creaking under his foot. "I'm not asking for coffee or anything. Although if you invite me, I'll pick you up and carry you inside for a night you won't forget."

"I had forgotten how persuasive you can be."

"I didn't forget how good you smell." He eye-stroked her. "Have I told you how much I like the scent of flowers on you?" He dipped his head. "Taking you to that restaurant was as much for me as it was for you."

"Dinner was nice and I appreciate that you picked a spot to win me over, but I don't like being manipulated. Your honesty calls out to me more than anything."

A grin creased the corners of his eyes as they reached

the third floor. "I forget sometimes that you and I are in the same business."

"Just be straight with me."

"I can do that."

Could she believe him? Leaning back against her door, she searched his eyes for some sign of his deeper thoughts and feelings. She looked and found...passion.

Not a surprise, but unsettling all the same, with her own emotions in such a whirl that she felt the least upset could send her spinning. Before she could think, she reached to dust melting snowflakes off the lapel of his jacket. Hard, male muscles twitched under her touch. Her pulse raced, stirring that pottery wheel inside her faster.

"Whoa!" She jolted back, pressing a hand to her belly.

Frowning, Jason braced a palm against her back. "Are you all right? Give me the key. You need to lie down."

"I'm fine, totally fine." She stepped away before she succumbed to the temptation to lean against him. The baby's swift kick brought her back to reality. "Our kiddo is just exercising off that fabulous chicken marsala."

His gaze dropped to her stomach. His fingers flexed. The way he didn't ask for what he so obviously wanted nudged her to offer. "Do you want to feel?"

He nodded curtly.

She took his hand and flattened it to the spot where... "I'm not sure if you'll be able to feel—it's still kinda early." And no way was she inviting him to touch her bare stomach. Would he be at her doctor appointments down the road? Too much to think about. She needed to stay in the moment, one thing at a time. "Wait, just a little to the left." She guided him. "Right there."

His eyes widened. He looked up at her quickly, then back to her stomach. "I think I... Yeah. Wow."

"Sometimes I just lie in bed and feel the baby move until all of the sudden I see an hour has passed. Wild, isn't it?"

"I had no idea what that felt like. I've never..." He looked up at her again, holding her gaze, no shutters in place for the first time. "Thank you."

All noise around her faded, the other couple, the barking poodle, became a dull din drowned out by the drum of her pulse in her ears. She linked her fingers with his, wondering what it would be like to follow this attraction.

The heels on her boots brought her closer to his face. He only needed to duck a little, or she could arch up. Only a kiss. Nothing more. A simple...brush of his mouth against hers. She could feel his breath already touching her in a phantom caress and, God, how she wanted this, just this much. Why even bother worrying about whether they would take it further?

She nipped his bottom lip. He growled low, then took her mouth with his, fully, no way to tell who'd opened for whom first because the hunger just took over. They'd kissed in her office before landing on the sofa. It hadn't been a totally impersonal hookup, but they certainly had made out. Not like this, standing in the hall outside her door, necking with the man who'd taken her to dinner. There was something wonderfully romantic about it. Something that made her want to sink in for a while and just enjoy the moment.

Her fingers tested the texture of his short hair still damp from snowflakes. He smelled of the cool crisp winter air and a hint of oregano from the restaurant, and her ravenous senses lapped up every bit.

"Lauren," he whispered, scattering kisses up her cheekbone, over her ear, "this is getting more than a little out of control for a public hallway. Do you want to move inside?"

Did she? She inched back to stare up into his face.

Her apartment door swept open, startling her back a step and into the present. Jason stepped in front of her protectively, his back tense under her fingers. When had she touched him again? Her fingers curled deeper into the fabric of his jacket, taut muscles flexing under her grip.

She peered over his shoulder and winced. "Mom?"

# Four

Lauren stared at her mother, framed in the open doorway, and tried not to panic. How long would it take those keen maternal eyes to notice the baby bulge under the baggy sweater? She really should have taken care of informing her parents before now.

Second-guessing herself served no good. She needed to focus on how to best handle the moment, which began with gauging her mother's current mood by how she dressed.

Jacqueline Presley had always been a strange mix of junior league meets avant garde. She wore her standard Chanel suit—plum purple today—but with chunky jewelry in an animal theme. A family of ruby lizards climbed up one side of her jacket. Her emerald cape with silver fringe was draped haphazardly over her arm. She must have just arrived.

How she'd talked her way past the super to get inside, Lauren didn't even want to know.

She had more pressing concerns, anyway. Her mother's clothes said she was in an up mood, but her tousled hair, chipped nails and shaking hands testified to a frenetic edge. Sure, they were minor signs, but Lauren had learned long ago to catalog every detail, read the nuances, prepare herself for anything.

As she struggled for what to say, Jason stepped forward and thrust out his hand. "Hello, Mrs. Presley. I'm Jason Reagert."

"Reagert?" She shook his hand, then tapped the air with a rhinestone-studded fingernail, chewed down on one corner. "Are you related to J. D. Reagert of Reagert Comm?"

His smile tightened but didn't disappear. "My father, ma'am."

"Oh, no need to call me *ma'am*. I'm Jacqueline." She took his arm and hauled him into the apartment, not even looking back at Lauren.

What the hell?

She'd been so freaked out worrying that her mother would learn about the baby—only to be ignored completely. But then, Jason represented everything her mother wanted in a son-in-law. Lauren followed them inside, closing the door behind her.

Jacqueline's laugh bounced around in the vaulted ceiling. Her mom had many wonderful qualities, and she could certainly be charming when she wanted. And the times she'd taken meds, life had been level, happy. Lauren couldn't quite say "normal," because her mother was always quirky and artsy, but when she took care of her health, those eccentricities were actually fun.

God, she hoped this was one of those times.

Lauren inched her purse around over her stomach and followed Jason and her mother deeper into the apartment, the pair still with their backs to her. Jason pulled out a chair for her mother at the dining table. Odd choice, but Lauren wasn't going to argue, since sitting at the wooden ice-cream-parlor-style table would conveniently hide her pregnancy.

Had Jason known that? A sharp and watchful edge in his eyes indicated he was very aware of everything going on around him. Realization washed over her. Jason was shielding her from her mother. He'd maneuvered everyone so Lauren's stomach was never visible, while keeping her mother distracted—offering to take her wrap, pulling out her chair, asking about her trip down.

Could they actually pull this off without her mom finding out about the baby in such an explosive way tonight? It looked increasingly possible as Jacqueline seemed enraptured with quizzing Jason about his new job in California. Neither of them spared so much as a glance across the table at Lauren. Jacqueline was too busy soaking up the attention to even fidget with her glasses chain dangling from her neck.

How strange, not to mention different, to have someone run interference with her mom. She'd never had that before—her father had been more concerned with hiding out than containing the situation. Okay by her. She was an adult now.

Still, it felt good to breathe. Of course, Jason offered

only a temporary reprieve. The news would come out soon enough, but in a more controlled setting.

Fifteen or so minutes of small talk later, Jason clasped Jacqueline's hand. "Jacqueline, it's been a delight meeting you. I hope you don't find me pushy here, but I've just gotten in from California to visit Lauren and have to leave soon…"

Her mother scooped up her cape and passed it to Jason to hold open for her. "Oh, don't let me keep you two lovebirds. I'll just head back to my suite at the Waldorf." Stepping into her cape and shaking out the fringe, she turned to Lauren. "Lunch, dear, you and I, as soon your guy here returns to California."

"Sure, Mom. We really do need to talk."

"I know a great place with all organic foods. It'll help you with that water retention. Your face is a little puffy." Jacqueline leaned close to press her cheek to Lauren's. "He's a keeper. Don't mess it up this time, dear."

Lauren secured her purse over her stomach. "Of course, Mom."

She so didn't want to have a conversation with her mom about finding an "acceptable catch," especially in front of Jason. She could even let the "puffy face" comment pass if it meant getting through this visit without a confrontation. Come to think of it, her mother would probably see this baby as an opportunity to reel in that "catch."

Lauren shivered in disgust at the thought of her child being used that way.

Jacqueline breezed toward the door with a wave over her shoulder but not even a backward glance at Lauren as Jason escorted her out to the hall.

Lauren sagged in the chair, her purse sliding to the hardwood floor with a hefty thump. She smoothed her hand over the slight bulge of her stomach, the baby rolling under her hand. No child of hers was going to be seen as merely an opportunity to climb up some social ladder.

A tear dripped off her chin.

Damn. She scrubbed the back of her wrist along her face. She hadn't even known she was crying. She heard the creak as Jason closed the door, and she swiped her fingers under her eyes again, praying she'd cleared away any mascara tracks.

As he stepped into the apartment again, she scavenged up a smile. "I can't even begin to thank you."

"For what?" He pulled a chair closer to her and sat.

"For running interference with Mom, for not saying anything about the baby or my slimy accountant."

"I'm all about making things easier for you and our baby."

Our baby.

His words sent a shiver through her. Of excitement or fear?

She thought of their kiss in the corridor and how quickly she could land right back in his arms again, in his bed. Jason had a way of making her lose control, and that scared her most of all.

Lauren clenched her hands together to keep from clasping his hand on the table. "You've been great. Really. Coming here the minute you found out, dinner, handling Mom." In so many other ways, but still she couldn't forget the past months of no communication, not even so much as an e-mail. They needed to talk about that night sometime. Discussing it seemed less daunting now in light of the land mine she'd just dodged with her mother. "You haven't asked how I ended up pregnant."

He scratched his jaw, leaning back. "I figured the condom must have failed."

Memories of their frantic coupling churned through her mind, her body still humming from their make-out session in the hallway. Four months ago they'd torn at each other's clothes. And yes, they'd kissed then, too, deeply, frantically, desperate to connect. Then the mad fumbling through his wallet to sheath him before... "We were pretty preoccupied at the time." Lauren shifted in her chair, suddenly unable to get comfortable. "I appreciate you not questioning me about it."

Her eyes lingered on his strong neck as she remembered the strength of it under her lips, savoring the bristly texture of his late-day shadow.

"We've known each other for a year and worked together most of the time the last month before I left. And I realize you weren't seeing anyone else around the time we, uh, landed on your office couch."

"I wasn't seeing you, either." Yet they'd ended up having impulsive sex, something she'd never done before. She'd only ever been with two men before, both long-term relationships, both men she'd considered marrying.

He angled closer, skimming his knuckles up and down her arm. "We may not have been dating, but I sure as hell always noticed you."

His stroking hand moved slower, shifting from soothing to sensual, the heat of his skin searing through her sweater. She wanted him so damn much.

Too much.

She inched out of reach before she did something impulsive like draw him down to the floor with her. God, why hadn't someone warned her about how out of control her hormones would be during pregnancy? Crying one minute and ready to jump Jason's bones the next.

He rested his hand back on the table, giving her the space she needed. Okay, she would need a couple of states between them to disperse the tangy scent of his aftershave.

Lauren cleared her throat, settling on a subject sure to douse any passion. "How did you manage that whole scene with my mother so perfectly?"

His eyes smoked over her, assessing for three very loud beats of her heart before he relaxed in his chair again.

"A while back," he said, apparently willing to concede her abrupt change of subject, "I landed an ad account for a new makeup line. The spokesmodel got pregnant. They still wanted her face on their product but not her stomach. We did some very inventive posing on that photo shoot."

"Well, I appreciate your help all the same." She toyed with a peppermill in the middle of the table. Maybe if she ground some flakes she could explain away the tears stinging behind her eyes. "I know I'm just delaying the inevitable."

He tugged a linen napkin out of the basket and passed it to her. "Telling your mother about her first grandchild should be a happy event—at a time and place of your choosing."

"Thank you for understanding." Taking the napkin from him, she dabbed at her eyes, cursing the hormonal flood yet again. The weight of everything going on overwhelmed her—from saving her company to being pregnant on her own. It all felt like too much and Jason had offered her help. What did she have to lose by going to California with him, just for a couple of weeks to get her world in order and work out logistics for their life as parents? "Okay, Jason."

"Okay what?"

She drew in a deep breath and crossed her fingers as the words bubbled out. "I'll go to California with you for two weeks and pretend to be your fiancée."

His eyes flashed with surprise briefly, then his face smoothed into his best calm-executive expression, which she'd seen him plaster in place often in the past. "Two weeks?"

So he'd caught that part. "I can't leave my business indefinitely." And she couldn't let herself get caught up in playing house with Jason. "Look what happened when I was out of the office for a few weeks because of the morning sickness. My slimy accountant ran off with half a million dollars."

"Valid point." His features hardened, more angular with his negotiating face. "And you're willing to accept my offer to infuse some cash into your business?"

"A loan. With interest and a payment plan." Her pride would only let her go so far with this crazy idea. "I wouldn't feel right otherwise, especially since I'm not agreeing to move to California permanently."

"We could consider the money an investment for our child."

"Jason, don't push your luck. Even if half a million dollars isn't much to you, it's the principle here."

"Fine," he conceded. "I hear you."

"I'll accept a low interest rate." She wouldn't allow her pride to push her to the point of bankruptcy again.

"Good business decision. I'm obviously not going to argue, since I would have given you the money."

"I'm going to be more careful this time in choosing who will watch over the business while I'm away. I considered hiring an office manager when the morning sickness first set in, but opted to cut corners to save money. That's a mistake I won't be repeating."

She'd gotten a second chance, one she couldn't afford to lose. Her baby deserved a strong, capable mother.

Lauren jabbed Jason in the chest with a finger. "But I really mean it when I say two weeks. I'm nervous enough being away from the office for that long."

"You come back to New York in two weeks, but we leave the engagement on the books to quiet your mom and my client." He clasped her finger and folded it against his chest, enfolding her in the warmth of his touch and chocolate-brown eyes.

"After a while, we can say time apart took its toll."

"Hey, we just became engaged." His thumb rasped along the inside of her wrist, her pulse leaping in response. "Do we have to plan the breakup already?"

"Quit trying to make me laugh." *And quit trying to turn me on.*

He linked their fingers, holding her as firmly with his molten brown gaze. "But you have the most beautiful smile. Call me a selfish bastard, but I like to see it."

The heat of his hand and his eyes stoked the barely banked fire inside her. She needed to hold strong.

Lauren eased her hand away. "I have one final condition."

"Name it. I'll make it happen."

Lauren clasped the arms of her chair to keep her hands off him and her resolve in place. "Under no circumstances will we be sleeping together again."

She'd agreed to go to California to give herself breathing room to regroup, to save her company and, yes, to help him secure his job. But she refused to let him blindside her a second time. She couldn't risk the way sex with Jason stole her ability to think straight.

As she stared at his broad shoulders and steamy brown eyes, she wondered if she'd cut off her nose to spite her face.

Jason had known he would win in the end. Still, he was damn glad to be pulling up to his home in San Francisco's Mission District with Lauren firmly planted in the seat next to him. Sure, she'd tossed that "no sex" clause into the agreement, a frustrating turn. Not unexpected, though. And not insurmountable. He'd seen the arousal in her eyes, the tightening of her nipples under her sweater.

He had hope.

Their day traveling together had gone well in a chartered flight with a catered supper on Sunday night. He'd bided his time and kept things low-key. He had two weeks to win her over, and he wasn't going to blow it on the first day by pushing too fast. Right now, he needed to focus on getting her settled into his restored Victorian house for the night as smoothly as possible.

The streetlamps brightened the inside of the sedan. Lauren pressed her hand to the window of his Saab, her eyes widening. "You have a house."

"I don't live in my car."

She laughed lightly, then looked back at the house as he drove around to the garage. "I just expected you to live in some cool condo in a singles' complex." She looked closer and gasped. "And look at that window box next door. They already have some flowers in January. This is all so...domestic."

He hadn't thought of it that way and wasn't sure he was comfortable with the label. He turned off the ignition and closed the garage door. "When I was in the Navy, I spent so much time on a cramped ship and on the road. I'm ready for a space of my own."

"Babies are noisy and take up lots of room."

"Unless you're pregnant with a dozen sailors, I don't think we're going to have a problem with space." Winking, he stepped out of the car and opened the door for her, leading her out to the covered walkway connecting the new garage to the historic, million-dollar home.

He'd bought the property for its location. As he walked up the steps to the side entrance, he saw the details anew through Lauren's artistic eyes—an old remolded Victorian home, gray with white trim. Hardwood floors stretched throughout, the newly refinished sheen gleaming as he flicked on the lights. Crown molding and multipaned stained-glass windows had made it too good an investment to pass up.

"This is absolutely gorgeous." She spun on her heel, her loose dress swirling around her calves. Her pinup-girl curves and beauty sucker punched him.

Jason loosened his tie. "I like being at the center of things."

"Does that mean you're not a workaholic anymore?"

She skimmed her fingers along the marble fireplace mantel, her gaze skipping around the room with obvious appreciation.

He'd known the vintage home would appeal to her. He hadn't been shopping for the two of them when he'd bought the house, but appreciated the dumb luck of owning a home she liked. Or would that qualify as having something in common?

"My time for recreation is very limited. Having restaurants and nightlife more accessible makes sense."

She traced the chair rail down the hall. "What a find."

He set her luggage at the foot of the stairs. "The couple who lived here before remodeled the whole place, wiring and all. They even gutted and updated the kitchen and baths."

"So how did you luck into it?" Her auburn hair swished along her back as she looked over her shoulder at him.

"Apparently the renovations put a strain on their marriage and they ended up in divorce court. It looked like they broke up in the middle of a project. The upstairs guest bath still had the materials for wallpaper stripping set up in the tub." He'd been working so hard landing the Prentice account, he'd only gotten around to clearing out that guest bathroom the week before. "Neither of them could afford to keep the house on their own, so they sold it."

"How sad." She wrapped her arms around her waist, accentuating her lush curves. "Don't you worry about stepping into all that bad karma?"

"I would worry more about paying the extra cash to get the same house down the road."

"I guess so," she said, her soft voice bouncing around the nearly empty space. "What about furniture?"

He glanced at the bare walls and mostly vacant rooms. A few moving boxes were stacked in a corner in each room. He just pulled out what he needed as he needed it. "I haven't had time to pick anything out and my old place came furnished. So once I got here, I bought the bare basics and went to work. I figured I might as well wait to do it right rather than buy a bunch of crap I regret later on." He gestured for her to follow him. "Come on back to the kitchen. I have seats and food."

"You could hire a decorator." Her footsteps echoed down the hall on her way into the kitchen. Her gasp of pleasure at the spacious layout made him smile.

"I can wait. I have everything I need." He steered her toward one of the two bar stools at the mammoth island between the kitchen and eating area. "A recliner, a big TV. There's a bed upstairs with a top-of-the-line mattress."

Her lips went tight as she sat, resting her elbows on the Brazilian-granite countertop. "Where will I be sleeping?"

"In my bed of course." His temperature spiked at just the words. He opened the refrigerator. "Bottled water? Fruit?"

"Yes, please." She stood and took the drink and grapes from him. "Then I hope for your sake that your guest room has a comfy bed or sofa."

God, he loved the way she didn't take his bull, just quietly lobbing the serve back to him. "No furniture there, either. I'll sleep in the recliner for now and have another mattress delivered."

"That really sucks for you tonight, because I am not

going to feel sorry for you and invite you to share the bed." She tipped back her water.

"You're heartless." He slid a hand behind her waist and brought a grape to her lips.

"I'm fairly certain I made myself clear about the sleeping arrangements before we left New York." She plucked the grape from his hands and popped it into her mouth.

"Can't blame a guy for trying." His thumb stroked along her spine as he watched her eyes for any signs of arousal—like the widening of her pupils, the pulse along her neck quickening.

"Jason, we can't just sleep together for a couple of weeks and then have a civil relationship. It's not logical. We have a child to think about. We can't afford to take risks."

Since she hadn't shoved him away, he urged her a little closer until she stood between his knees. "Don't you think our kid would like to see us together?"

"Are you suddenly magically ready for a long-term relationship? Because you damn well weren't prepared for that four months ago."

His eye twitched. "Sure, why not?"

"How charming." Her lip curled. She shoved his arms away and charged toward the stairs.

"Hey, I'm trying here." He spread his arms wide, following. "This is uncharted territory for me, too."

She gripped her roll bag. "I'm going to bed. Alone. Enjoy your recliner."

Not a problem, since he doubted he would sleep, anyway.

"I will. Thanks. I'm a deep sleeper." He slid the

suitcase from her hand. "And I'm also a guy who can't watch a woman—especially a pregnant woman—lug a suitcase up the stairs."

Without another word, he loped ahead of her. He had her in his house and he had two weeks to work his way into her bed. And once he got there? He intended to make sure she wasn't so quick to boot him out again.

# Five

Loneliness echoed around her in the empty bedroom.

Lauren slumped against the closed door, Jason's footsteps growing softer as he made his way to his recliner. Sure, she jammed too much furniture and plant life into her apartment back in Manhattan, but this space? It was beyond sparse.

A mattress on a frame.

One brass side table for a lamp and alarm clock.

And a closet full of clothes hanging from the racks and neatly folded on the shelves.

She pitched her purse on the bed, the bag bouncing to rest on the brown-and-blue comforter. Again the ring rolled out like a bad penny that kept turning up. Lauren placed it on the brass table. The generic piece of furniture.

Damn it, she didn't want to feel sorry for him. Jason

was known as a shark in the business world, and stakes were too high for her to be caught unawares. But something about this place made her sad, made her want to bring flowers and color and noise to his world.

His whole house looked forlorn, for that matter, all the sadder given the home absolutely shouted out for love and attention, parties and family. Although he did have two bar stools in the kitchen. Had they come with the place or had be bought them with the notion of entertaining someone?

Kneeling, she unzipped her suitcase and pulled out the silky nightshirt that still fit. But for how much longer? She smoothed a hand over the growing curve of her stomach. Certainly not femme fatale material.

Her eyes scanned the empty walls, the barren bay window that cried out for a pair of comfy chairs, perfect for a couple watching a sunrise together. But other than those bar stools, it didn't appear he'd brought anyone here.

Anyone except her.

He knew she hadn't been dating anybody for the last six months he'd lived in New York—but *he* had been. Well, up until a couple of months before he'd left, that was. She wouldn't have slept with a guy who was seeing someone else, no matter how swept up into the attraction she may have felt.

Lauren peeled off her travel-weary clothes and slid the nightshirt over her head. The silky fabric teased her breasts to pebbly peaks, leaving her achy. Wanting. God, it would be so easy to walk down those stairs and satisfy the ache between her legs.

She eyed the door and actually considered taking

what she wanted. She even stepped forward. Her toe hooked on the strap to her computer bag.

Her computer. Her work. She needed to remember her reason for coming here in the first place—to give herself time to plan, to save her business, to save her pride.

Too bad a laptop and pride made for very chilly bedfellows.

Jason stepped over the serpentine computer cord, Lauren's laptop closed and resting on the bedside table by his alarm clock. The ring box sat by the clock, closed. Her ring finger was still bare. She'd agreed to be his fiancée, even flown to California, but she hadn't committed one hundred percent to the plan.

He set the breakfast tray on the corner of the mattress and took his time studying the sleeping woman in his bed. Her auburn hair was spread over the brown cotton pillowcase, the sheets tangled around her legs. Her lemon-yellow nightshirt rucked up to the top of her thighs. He remembered well how soft those legs were to the touch, how strong when wrapped around his waist, insistently urging him along. Keeping his hands to himself with her in his space all the time was going to be tougher than he'd expected, but the game went to those who were patient.

Jason sat on the edge and indulged himself by stroking her hair away from her face. He hated to disturb her, but also didn't want to leave her alone in a strange place without checking on her. "Wake up, sleepyhead."

She rolled to her back and stretched, the nightshirt pulling taut over the growing curve of her stomach.

Feeling the baby move the other day had been...amazing. And unsettling.

Persuading Lauren to stay became all the more important.

Her eyes flickered open, vague and unfocused. She smiled, reaching up to him, and just that damn fast he forgot about careful plans and brushed a kiss over each beautiful eye. Her soft skin enticed him to hang around a while longer, kiss the tip of her nose, her chin. He would have liked to work his way lower, but she wasn't fully awake yet, and he wanted her aware and consenting the next time they had sex.

She wriggled slowly, sensuously, beneath him, waking him up hard and fast, harder still as she sighed sweetly. He rested his forehead against hers.

And then she froze, her eyes snapping open wide. "Jason—" she shoved at his chest and slid to the side "—I thought I told you to stay out of my bed."

He eased back, frustration pulsing through his veins. *Patience.* "You're in *my* bed, remember?"

"A technicality." She tugged her nightshirt down to her knees with one hand and pulled the sheet up higher with her other.

"I remember you being more of a morning person." He lifted the black lacquer tray from the corner of the bed.

"That was back when my stomach didn't live in my throat." She eyed the breakfast tray packed with juice, milk, toast and eggs. "Thanks, though. This is nice of you."

"I'm sorry you're not feeling well."

"I'm better now. At least I can keep food down." She plucked up a piece of toast and nibbled at the corner.

Content she was going to eat, he stood, for the first time in...well, ever wanting to delay leaving for the office. "I'll be back at lunchtime."

"You don't need to. I can entertain myself." She sipped her milk. "I have work on the computer and calls to make."

"All right, then. We'll meet up for supper. Tomorrow I need to introduce you to my boss, and there's a big shindig in the evening later this week."

"Ah, so I'll get to meet the people who don't like the fact that you have a pregnant girlfriend." She scrunched her slim nose. "Great. I can't wait."

"Actually it's the client who has the problem, not my coworkers." He tugged a tie out of the closet, slid it under his collar and began knotting it.

"Oh, that's right. The old-fashioned guy."

He flipped his collar back in place and reached for his suit jacket, the intimacy of the morning stealing over him and she'd only been in his house one night. "It's his money to spend how he chooses. If we want his account—and we do—then we have to play by his rules, especially with Golden Gate Promotions nipping at our heels. Surely the businesswoman inside you understands that."

"I hear what you're saying."

"It would really help convince people to buy into our engagement if you would wear this." He scooped the ring box off the table and placed it on her breakfast tray. Winning a point was all about the presentation. If he offered her the diamond nestled in his palm, it seemed too much like a real proposal. Hopefully, by casually dropping it on the tray, she would feel less crowded.

Lauren nudged the box with the tip of her index

finger. "You can't really expect to marry someone just to please a business associate."

Her question churning in his brain, he decided honesty would work best. She was smart and insightful, two things he enjoyed most about her.

"Honestly, Lauren, I'm not sure how far I would go with this. I'm still taking things a day at a time, working to make the best decision possible to secure the baby's future, which means smoothing out your world and mine. Making the engagement as official as possible—including flashing this ring around—will go a long way toward taking care of those concerns. It could keep your mother off your back for a while, too."

Lauren lightly punched his arm. "Now you're playing dirty pool."

"I'm a man on a mission." He tapped the little velvet box.

She hugged her knees and stared at the ring as if it was a bomb, not a three-carat, flawless rock.

Nice. He restrained the urge to laugh. Especially since it really wasn't all that funny.

Lauren tore her eyes from the ring. "What will I say if someone asks when we're getting married?"

He cricked his neck from side to side, working out the stress already knotting its way up and it wasn't even seven o'clock yet. "Tell them your mother is planning the wedding. Tell them we're looking for a date that fits in with our work schedules. Tell them we're thinking about bolting to Vegas and will keep them posted."

She scooped up the box and held the ring so it reflected the morning light streaming through the stained-glass window. "You're really, really good at lying."

Lying? He prided himself on being a man who stuck to the truth, even if he did his best to make that truth something others would buy into. "I'm just an ad man spinning the product."

She stayed silent, but her eyes said loud and clear she thought he was lying to himself.

Steam from the shower still coating the air, Lauren tucked the towel more snugly around her body and raced to the telephone. God, she felt like a teenager rushing to catch a call from a guy.

Gasping, she snatched up her cell phone from the bedside table, her wet hair a dripping rope over her shoulder. "Hello?"

Her mother's voice popped through the airwaves, loud, high-pitched and frantic. "Lauren, I got a call from the lawyer for Aunt Eliza's estate today."

Lauren dropped to the edge of the bed, her stomach knotting as she mentally kicked herself for not checking caller ID. "Why is he speaking with you, instead of phoning me directly?"

Could something actually be wrong? The money from Aunt Eliza's estate had already been transferred to her—and stolen by the crooked accountant.

"He said he's looking for you and can't find you. Where are you?"

"I'm on a business trip, but I have my cell phone and am checking e-mail. I'll give him a call. Thank you for the heads-up," she said quickly, hoping to end the conversation.

"Dear, he says you're having financial troubles."

Lauren measured her words carefully. Her parents

had plenty of money and didn't hesitate to share it with her, which was generous. Except that money came with big strings attached. And quite frankly, she didn't want to be a trust-fund kid, living her entire life off Mom and Dad's hard work, never accomplishing anything on her own. "Things are tight at work, but I'm settling that out."

"Tight? Most businesses fail in their first year, you know, dear." Her mom's jeweled glasses chain clicked in the background as she fidgeted.

"Yes, Mother. I know the statistics." And she prayed her business wouldn't add to the failed numbers on that list. "Thank you for passing along the message."

Jacqueline pressed ahead. "You know, I'm going to call my accountant to talk to you. Make sure to keep your cell phone with you."

"Thank you, Mom, but I can handle it." And she would. She hugged her towel closer, shivering.

"You've never been good with money, dear."

Staying silent, she bit her lip. Hard. The barb dug deeper than her teeth.

Her mother continued. "Remember when you blew your entire savings on that watch?"

"Mom—" the words bubbled up in spite of the fact she knew better than to argue with her mom on a rant "—I was in the third grade. My savings fit in a piggy bank."

Her mother's voice cracked on the start of a sob. "Of course. What do I know? I only care about you." Jacqueline gasped again and again between words, her voice bobbling. "There's no need to attack me. You're just like your father, always picking, picking, picking at everything I do."

"Mom, I'm sorry—"

"Yes, well, at least I have somewhere to go to relieve the stress. Did I tell you about my new vacation home?"

Lauren closed her eyes. Already weary and it wasn't even lunchtime. Her mother's mood swings were nothing new, but exhausting all the same. She just listened and hmmmed when her mother shared the details of the latest perfect place to get away to.

Which actually meant a new place to start over, since she'd alienated the people in her old vacation community. Lauren had seen it play out time and time again. While she half listened to her mother, she stared at the little velvet box.

Jason had been so calmly helpful in dealing with her mother. He'd helped her with her business troubles and her mother. He was certainly trying to understand what *she* needed, as well, even down to small details like the flowers in her office and the toast for the morning.

His reasons for becoming engaged might feel calculated, but what did she really have to lose by simply wearing his ring? Just by sliding that diamond on her finger, she could help him secure his job, which made for a more secure future for their baby. He was already doing everything he could to help stabilize her business, too.

She slipped the velvet box from the side table. The ring winked suggestively from the bed of velvet.

It was just a formality, really. She was here, in his house, pregnant with his child. What did it matter if she wore the ring?

Phone tucked under her chin, Lauren slid the ring in place and closed her fist. She knew this was the right thing to do, but the thought of sitting around here all day staring at that ring and second-guessing herself made her nerves churn so fast she feared losing her toast.

Jason wanted his office to know about their engagement. He'd given her time to gain her footing even though the delay could cost him. So why bother waiting? She could meet the people he worked with and even surprise Jason with a casual meal out where they could start on their path of a smoother relationship for the baby's sake.

Decision made, she stood. "Mom, it's been great talking to you, but I have a lunch date I just can't miss."

Staring out the taxi window, Lauren took in the towering white buildings of Union Square's posh shopping district. Somewhere in that concrete jungle with palm trees waited Maddox Communications. She'd done more research on the Internet about MC before leaving Jason's house. She was a businesswoman in her own right and knew to arm herself as well as possible before entering any new camp.

The Maddox patriarch, James, had founded Maddox Communications more than fifty years ago. He'd married Carol Flynn and they'd had two sons: Brock and Flynn, who each went into the family business. When James died eight years ago, Brock took over the helm, with his brother acting as vice president.

Lauren leaned forward, reading signs, watching for Powell Street, and, more important, the building referred to as The Maddox. Finally the cab cruised to a stop in front of the seven-story, Beaux Arts–style building constructed in 1910. The article she'd found said the building had been set for demolition when James

Maddox saved it from the wrecking ball and had it lovingly restored in the late seventies.

Now the building was reputed to be worth ten times his purchase price.

She tipped the cabbie and stepped out of the taxi. Automatic doors whooshed wide. The first floor was home to the trendy New American cuisine restaurant Iron Grille and several retail stores. At the elevator, she consulted the building legend and found the second and third floors were rented out to other businesses.

Floors five and six were the corporate offices. Directions indicated that clients and visitors to Maddox Communications should enter the offices on the sixth floor.

Elevator Muzak piped jazz horns, floors chiming smoothly and quickly. The elevator opened directly to a reception desk and total opulence and edginess, from the black-stained oak floors to the stark white walls with original art. Two seventy-inch plasma screens sat on either side of the large reception desk, showing videos/commercials with a small scroll of words along the bottom proclaiming they'd been produced by Maddox Communications.

Jason had landed well in his new job. A sense of pride in his accomplishment beyond his parents' wealth stirred. She sure understood how tough it could be to step out of the shadow of influential parents to make your own mark in the world.

Lauren's low heels clicked along the high-sheened floors.

The receptionist smiled. "Welcome to Maddox Communications." Her short brown hair swished with every perky twitch of her head. "How can I help you?"

Lauren glanced down at the woman's name plate—Shelby—and smiled. "Hello, Shelby, I'm here to see Jason Reagert. My name's Lauren Presley."

"Yes, ma'am, if you'll wait over there?" She gestured to the large white leather sofas.

Lauren flickered her thumb over the engagement ring nervously as butterflies stirred. Shelby eyed her with undisguised curiosity. Lauren's stomach flipped again.

Suddenly Lauren wasn't so sure this had been a good idea, after all. What kind of game had she been expecting to play? She'd wanted to show Jason she was in charge and had only succeeded in looking erratic.

She cringed inside. Maybe she should just leave. She inched her purse around to cover her stomach, starting to stand.

A shadow stretched from the hall and she hesitated. Was it Jason already?

A lean man, around forty with black hair, came into sight, stern and very obviously not Jason. The man stopped at the desk, passing a note, his voice low. Lauren decided to make her big escape—

Shelby whispered back and pointed to Lauren. He straightened and walked toward her. Damn.

He extended his hand. "Hello, I'm Brock Maddox." The CEO. The big boss and obviously one confident son of a gun. "I understand you're here to see our wonderboy."

Busted. She shook his hand. "Lauren Presley. I'm a friend of Jason's. I'm also a graphic designer. We worked together on a couple of projects back in New York."

He eyed her stomach briefly. Sheesh. Was it that obvious? Apparently so. "Are you in San Francisco on work or vacation?"

"Both," she answered noncommittally. "Shelby was just about to let Jason know I'm here."

"Follow me. You can surprise him." Brock gestured over his shoulder and began plowing deeper into the Maddox offices, making low small talk she barely registered.

She was committed now to seeing this through. She quelled her nerves as he stopped in front of a door with a brass plate: Jason Reagert.

Inhaling a bracing breath, she pushed open the door and stopped short. Jason stood with his back to her—with a woman. *A smiling, stunningly beautiful red-haired woman who had her hand placed intimately on his arm.*

Fluttering nerves morphed into stone-still anger and a possessiveness that unnerved her to the tips of her toes.

He couldn't actually be seeing someone else? For a guy who cared about causing a scandal at work, he sure was playing with fire on a lot of levels.

Lauren stiffened her spine, feeling as frozen as the chill seeping into her heart. As she took in the couple standing together in his sleek office full of nautical prints, she couldn't believe she'd actually allowed herself to be hopeful simply because he'd brought her some toast and milk.

God, she was too easy. She'd had it with passively letting people walk all over her—her mother, her accountant, now Jason. She twirled the ring on her finger. At least she'd gotten a wake-up call when it came to the father of her baby.

He'd brought her here, damn it. And she wasn't going to scamper off like some scared rabbit. He wanted a fiancée? He was about to get one. Big-time.

"Hey there, lover." Lauren rested her hands on her stomach. "I'm absolutely starving. Are you ready for lunch?"

# Six

Damn it all.

Jason stepped back from Celia so her hand fell from his arm—something he'd been a second away from doing, anyway, right before Lauren walked into his office. What was she even doing here? And to make matters worse, Brock stood just behind her, scowling.

What rotten timing all the way around. Celia had stopped by his office to ask if he was going out for drinks after work, and he'd been preparing the words to clear the air between them when the door had opened.

He needed to do some damage control ASAP.

Lauren stepped farther into the office, her green eyes flashing like kryptonite, ready to take down Clark Kent. Her loose-fitting teal-colored dress swirled around her legs, brushing against her curves. The woman was total sensual confidence. She thrust out her hand—her left one—engagement ring glinting. "I'm Lauren Presley, Jason's fiancée just in from New York. We're getting married tonight."

"Married?" Celia squeaked.

"Tonight?" Jason needed air because keeping up with the surprises Lauren dished his way was an Olympic sport.

Brock cocked an eyebrow and leaned deeper into the doorway for a front-row seat.

Lauren breezed up to Jason's desk and hooked her arm in his. "I know an elopement is supposed to be a secret. Sorry for spilling the beans, honey, but I'm just so darn excited. We're catching a hop to Vegas. Hokey, I know, but, well—" she caressed her stomach "—it's obvious we don't have a whole lot of time to plan unless I want to get married wearing a tent."

Brock stuffed his hands into his pockets, his face inscrutable. "We all had no idea. Congratulations."

Jason adjusted his tie. "Thank you."

Lauren smiled apologetically. "Blame me for that secrecy part, Mr. Maddox. I tend to be very private about my social life. I'm working on being more open." She smiled up at Jason, her fingernails digging trenches into his arm, the only indication her joy was anything other than authentic. "Did you tell them you'll be late for work tomorrow?"

He patted her hand, easing her nails away. "Uh, not yet."

Brock straightened. "Sounds like you two have some plans to make. We all look forward to celebrating with you when you get back. Congratulations again." He held the door open for wide-eyed Celia to follow.

Man, Jason owed her an apology. But he also owed Lauren his loyalty. Had she been serious about eloping? If so, why the sudden change of heart?

Once the door clicked shut, Jason turned to Lauren, eyeing her warily. Her hand rested mighty darn close to the pewter antique compass he used as a paperweight. Was she the kind of person who threw things? She was usually so calm he wouldn't expect behavior like that from her. Although he also wouldn't have expected her to announce to the world they were jetting off to Vegas in a few hours.

He closed the gap between them, watching her stoic face for the least sign of her mood. "Were you serious about eloping tonight?"

"Serious as a heart attack." She set the pewter paperweight down with an extra-hefty thud.

"That's great, really great." He wasn't sure what had caused her change of heart. Hell, he wasn't sure what had propelled her to come to the office in the first place, but he didn't intend to argue. He brushed her hair back over her shoulder, lightly, intimately. "You have nothing to be jealous about with Celia."

"Who said I'm jealous?" she snapped.

"You're obviously upset." He cupped the back of her neck, massaging, hopefully soothing.

She shrugged free of his hand. "I don't like being made a fool of."

"There's nothing going on between Celia and me." And there wasn't.

"Does she know that?" Lauren jabbed a finger toward the door.

"I was making sure when you walked in."

Her eyes narrowed. "So there *is* something between the two of you."

"Whoa, hold on. Let's back this up." His feet damn near paced the shine off the black floors. "You're confusing the hell out of me. I try my ass off to charm you, and you all but toss my ring in the Bay. But when you think I'm flirting with another woman—which I was not—you're ready to elope?"

"As soon as you can pack your bags and book the flight." She closed the gap between them, blocking his pacing. Her jaw jutted aggressively. Which also happened to thrust out her full, kissable bottom lip.

She was hot when she was mad. Her eyes glimmered and her hair all but crackled from the heat radiating off her.

He was trying to do the straight-up best thing for their baby, and she was jerking him around nonstop. "If you're so pissed at me, why did you announce to the world we're headed to a Vegas wedding chapel?"

"Before—" she inched closer, tipping her head back until there was only a whisper of static-charged air between them "—I was worried about our feelings getting tangled up. But believe me, you've laid to rest all my fears about broken hearts and muddying the waters with an emotional train-wreck marriage like my parents went through. Now I know without question, there's not a chance in hell that I could fall in love with you. So let's go to Vegas."

Lauren held it together all the way through the introductions to Maddox Communications employees as Jason escorted her to his car. At least Jason had seemed to get the message she didn't want to give anything other than simple yes and no answers as he chartered a flight to Vegas.

She even managed to stay dry-eyed during the flight and through the sham of a wedding ceremony, difficult as hell to do since Jason had somehow managed to find a garden chapel service.

"I now pronounce you husband and wife. You may kiss the bride." The wedding chapel official closed his book of vows, running his hand over the floral cover. His Hawaiian shirt was a little over-the-top, but there were flowers and plants everywhere, just as she would have wanted, which made her all the more emotional.

Jason brushed her lips with a kiss, nothing overly dramatic and yet still perfect. Although the feel of his mouth against hers, even closed and only lightly touching, sent heat sparkling through her veins.

And made tears prick her eyes.

He palmed her waist gently, his thumb stroking so lightly but enough to send her spine arching toward him. Her stupid, stupid traitorous body.

She broke away, looking down quickly, needing space. "Excuse me."

Lauren raced to the washroom, desperate to leave before she embarrassed herself by falling completely apart in front of Jason. The whole day had been like a ride on a high-speed roller coaster, with more than a few loops tipping her life upside down. And somehow she'd zipped right along with it, never once calling for a halt, or even a slow down.

What in the world had she just done?

Lauren rushed into the restroom, potted palms and hanging ferns packing the space. She sank onto the rattan sofa and yanked tissues from the box on the end table. Finally she let the tears flow, tears she'd bottled up since the minute she'd found out she would be having a baby alone. Tears collected from worry about how all of this would affect her mother. Tears over the possibility of losing her business.

And tears over Jason?

This was her wedding night and as much as she wished she could allow herself to enjoy the fringe benefits without worry, she simply couldn't throw caution to the wind that easily.

She would do what it took to save her business. And yes, she would help Jason advance in his career, as well, because that was in the best interest of her child. Once this farcical marriage was done, she was through with Jason Reagert.

But first, she had to get through her wedding night.

Jason had a backlog of work waiting on his laptop propped by his seat on the plane. Normally flights made for the perfect time to play catch-up, and the pilot had just given them the all clear to use electronics.

Tonight he had no interest in what waited on that hard drive.

He shifted in the large leather chair, the aircraft droning softly through the dark, and studied his new bride reclined in a seat, talking on the plane's phone. She'd just finished telling her father about their elopement, making him swear not to tell Jacqueline that he'd been called first.

And although this wasn't a traditional wedding night by any measure, that didn't stop him from aching to share a good old-fashioned honeymoon suite with Lauren.

The single-engine plane offered enough room to move around and a small galley kitchen, but no sleeping quarters other than the chairs that reclined all the way back.

His wife—he paused at the surprise jolt to his pulse at just the word—dialed again and pressed the phone to her ear. She tucked her legs up to the side, adjusting the folds of her teal-colored dress.

"Hey, Mom," Lauren said, fine lines of stress and exhaustion fanning from the corners of her eyes. "Sorry to bother you so late, but I've got some really important news." Her gaze flicked over to him briefly, brushing him like the tips of a flame crackling over his body. "Remember Jason Reagert... Right...you met him at my place last week. Well, he's actually more than a friend. We just got married in Vegas...."

Jason thumbed the simple gold band on his finger. The wedding chapel had supplied it at the last minute, and he figured the ring would only help cement their case. He hadn't expected to notice its weight quite so much.

Lauren continued, nodding. "Yeah, Mom, I know you would have liked a heads-up so you could attend. But, uh, prepare yourself for more amazing news. Time was kinda tight for us. We're expecting a baby—"

A shriek sounded from the phone, followed by a long string of indistinguishable babbling. Lauren looked over at him briefly with a light wince before continuing. "I'm due in a little less than five months from now— No, I don't know the baby's gender yet— Uh, honeymoon? We have work..." She stopped, interrupted for what must have been the tenth time.

"Mom, that's really—" Sighing, she squinted her

eyes closed while the voice on the other end rambled louder and louder.

Jason took the phone from her hand. Lauren gasped, but he wasn't backing down. "Jacqueline? This is your new son-in-law, Jason, and I'm about to assert my marital rights. We'll be turning off this phone until at least noon tomorrow."

"But wait—" Jacqueline interrupted.

Jason interrupted right back. "Good night, Jacqueline." He turned off the phone.

"Wow," Lauren said. "Just flat-out wow. I don't know how to thank you for making that easier for me."

He wanted to... Hell, he didn't know what he could do to shield her from this sort of fall-out. "Are you all right?"

She smiled shakily. "At least that's done now."

"But are you all right?" he pressed.

"Of course." She straightened, the effort of gathering her control so obvious and laborious he wanted to pull her to him.

Protect her.

But she radiated stand-back vibes.

Calling her parents really had her freaked out, beyond just tense family relations like he had. "What's really going on here?"

"I'm not sure what you mean." She toyed with her purse, avoiding his eyes.

"You're obviously stressed over that phone call." He stroked her chin, tipping her face toward his. "I realize your mother is, uh, wired rather tight, but I think I'm missing something."

"I might as well tell you. You'll find out, anyway, over the years since she's the grandmother of your baby." She gripped the armrests in white-knuckled fists. "My mom was diagnosed as bipolar at twenty-two."

Damn. Not at all what he'd been expecting. "I'm really sorry. All this time we've known each other and you've never mentioned it."

But then, he'd been equally dodgy about his own past, which probably accounted for why he'd never probed too deeply about hers.

She rolled her head along the rest to face him full on, her expression wry. "It's not the sort of thing to come up in the workplace or during after-hour drinks—'Hey, my mom's manic-depressive.'"

What if he'd taken the time to talk to her more over the past year, to really listen, beyond discussing work and exchanging lighthearted banter? Could they have reached a point earlier where she would have shared this with him? He had no way of knowing, since apparently it took a forced marriage to coerce her into opening up.

He hadn't dug more deeply before, but he'd be damned if he'd make the same mistake again. "You said she was diagnosed at twenty-two?"

"She's been in and out of a doctor's treatment for a long while." Only going when her husband pushed or her daughter pleaded. "There were some good times when I was kid. But the past couple of years, she's decided she doesn't want to take any more of it— therapy or meds." Lauren straightened the drape of her dress again and again, restoring order. "Don't get me wrong, I'm not whining. Growing up with those sorts of mood swings was difficult, sure, but I like to think I'm a stronger person for it."

He respected the way she tried to put a positive spin

on things, but he suspected Lauren had done that so often no one noticed when she needed help. "Still, it must have been beyond tough for you as a kid, never knowing what to expect."

She plucked at a stray thread on the hem of her dress, nibbling her bottom lip. "I used to worry I would be like her. Since she never seems to accept she has a problem, what if I'm just oblivious? I've even visited doctors—shrinks—to have myself evaluated."

"And what did they say?"

She hesitated, folding her hands in her lap and studying him intently, then smiling. "You don't look like you're ready to run for the door."

"Given we're in an airplane, that would be damn reckless."

Thank God, she laughed. The sound stroked over him, arousing him as much as her soft hands. Hell, everything about her seemed to turn him inside out lately. But he wouldn't let that distract him. Her vulnerable eyes said she needed something from him now, and he was determined not to come up short.

"Lauren—" he measured his words as carefully as he had in any million-dollar presentation "—I've worked with you for over a year and I haven't seen anything to lead me to believe you have similar issues. I may not have any kind of psych degree, but I do know enough about you to be sure if there was ever a problem, you would do everything possible to take care of it."

Her throat moved in a long swallow as she blinked back tears. "I appreciate that. I like to believe that about myself. But when people learn about her illness, I feel like they look at me differently, as if my feelings are discounted because I'm just—"

"Hey—" he reached for her hand, unable to resist touching "—I take you seriously." And he did, personally and professionally. He trusted his judgment and for a year he'd seen the depth of her stability. If anything, he wondered how to break through her calm stoicism.

"Thank you." Linking their fingers, she squeezed his hand, her engagement ring and wedding band glinting in the low lighting overhead. "So far the doctors have all said they see no signs of bipolar disease in me. It usually crops up in your teens and twenties. I know there are no guarantees, but you won't hear me complain about turning thirty."

"That must have been a relief to hear."

"More than you can imagine." She curved her hand over her stomach. "Although now I'm worrying all over again. What if I've passed along the gene to our child?"

How did he feel about it? He'd barely processed he had a kid on the way. His thoughts had been focused on securing the baby's future, luring Lauren to California, steering clear of a career crash for both of them.

There were so many aspects of his child's life to worry about. And there were some things he absolutely couldn't control. His energies were best spent focused on dealing with what he *could* control.

"You're aware. I'm aware. We'll watch and provide whatever help our kid needs if the occasion arises." He squeezed her hand, enjoying the way her pulse leaped under his thumb. Or was that his heartbeat kicking up a notch at the feel of her silky-soft skin? "Hell, I've got a family history full of diabetics and a sister with dyslexia. There are few families with perfect medical histories."

A tear trickled down her cheek. "God, you can be so wonderfully logical and sweet both at the same time."

"Sweet? That's a new one for me."

"Hey, I'm serious here." She slid her fingers free and cupped his face in her hands. "Somehow you knew just the right thing to say and I could tell you meant every word."

"Just this morning you told me I'm the consummate ad man, good at making the sale even if I have to lie." He wasn't sure why he would try to wave a damn red flag in front of her when she was finally seeing something worthwhile in him. Since when was he into self-sabotage?

And then it hit him. Lauren was too important to him to be anything but completely honest. Could it be that he wanted more than just this wedding night from her?

He forced his focus back on her words, tough to do when it felt like the deck was rolling under his feet even though he knew the plane was flying steady on.

Her hands caressed his face lightly. "Maybe I'm starting to trust my instincts more and my instincts are telling me you're a good man."

She pressed her lips to his.

Her fingers slid back into his hair and he angled his head sideways for a better, fuller fit. The soft give of her mouth against him stirred a barely banked fire. He'd wanted her—hell, dreamed about being with her—since that night in her office. As much as he'd tried to tell himself he was merely immersed in the mayhem of starting a new, high-powered job, no one caught his eye or attention the way she had.

The way she still did.

Lauren leaned into him, her amazing curves pressing close. He burned to get his hands on her again. Skin to skin, touching and traversing every dip and valley, watching her skin flush from wanting him.

Damn it, his hands were shaking.

She smiled against his mouth a second before she eased away. The kiss wasn't an invitation into her bed, but it was a step in the right direction.

"Good night, Jason," she whispered, her hands gliding off him as she settled into her seat again. Her lashes fluttered closed and that fast she was asleep.

He, on the other hand, was wide-awake on their wedding night. Jason adjusted his pants, not that it helped ease the pinch of erection straining at his fly. Not much he could do about that now. He'd been so focused on working that wedding band onto her finger and getting her into bed, he hadn't realized the tougher part was still ahead of him.

Keeping the ring in place.

# Seven

How would she just pick up her old life in a couple of weeks?

Lauren sagged onto the edge of the bed, alone on her wedding night. What was left of it, anyway. By the time the chartered flight had landed and Jason drove them back to the house, the sun was already fighting to break over the horizon, oranges and yellows painting a hazy glow in the distance. She would have liked to watch the dawn with him, but he was already showering before he left for the office—some unmissable meeting, he said, but he vowed to come home early. She'd assured him she had business calls and work on her computer.

Strange wedding day. Strange honeymoon. Yet neither of them could afford to take time off. They were both struggling to launch careers. It was silly to want something more.

Too restless to go back to sleep just yet, she kicked off her shoes and wandered back into the upstairs hall. She didn't dare go near where Jason showered. She wasn't sure she could resist the temptation to slide under the spray with him in his luxuriously remodeled bathroom. Everything she'd seen in the house thus far was top-of-the-line, from the kitchen to the three bathrooms, to the master suite with a sitting area. She hadn't checked out the other bedrooms, but suspected they were just as sleek.

She creaked open the room to the door next to the master suite. *Empty.* Just hardwood floors, intricate crown molding and a few packing boxes. The view would make it a lovely guest room.

The next room—equally as empty—had a domed ceiling that called to her fingers to create a little Sistine Chapel with angels for a nursery. Swallowing hard, she closed the door behind her.

One bedroom left. She opened the door and found he actually had furniture here. Not much. Just a cherry table with an elaborate computer, printer and fax machine set up. A tangle of wires led to a power bar on the floor.

A nautical scene scrolled across the screen. Jason had talked about being near recreation, but the only personal items she saw in his house were business suits and work materials. As much as she understood the satisfaction work could bring, a part of her itched to fill his house—his world—with more. Furniture. Plants.

Lazy mornings watching a sunrise.

Sunbeams eased thicker and stronger through the sheers in the window. She needed sleep, for the baby if not herself. She pivoted on her heel—

And stopped short when a frame on the wall snagged her attention. It couldn't be. She stepped back into the room, closer until she saw clearly. Her stomach tightened. Framed on the wall across from the desk...

...the pen-and-ink drawing of a sailboat for a cologne campaign, a drawing created by her.

Her hand shaking, she traced the edges of the image and thought back to how he'd left her office without any argument, hadn't called in four months. Yes, she'd told him to leave, she'd pushed him away.

But could he have been thinking about her just as often as she'd dreamed of him?

Later that day in the MC boardroom, Jason wasn't any closer to figuring out how to keep Lauren in San Francisco. He seesawed his pen on the large oval acrylic table, turning the red leather chair ever so slightly from side to side.

Fellow ad exec Gavin Spencer eyed his rocking pen and raised an eyebrow.

Jason stilled. Damn. He felt like a kid hyped up on a pack of Pixy Stix, all because he wanted to be home with his new wife.

Instead, he was stuck at a mandatory meeting at work. Located in the center of the sixth floor, the boardroom was a huge space, with all four walls made of clear glass that turned opaque with the touch of a button. One wall was currently lit up as a huge screen for the computer-generated presentation of the day.

Brock clicked away the final image on his PowerPoint presentation before turning to the table again. "That's all for now." He turned to his assistant, Elle Linton. "You'll forward the specs from my presentation to everyone?"

She nodded efficiently, her brown hair clasped back smoothly and unpretentiously. "Will do, Mr. Maddox."

Brock tapped the button, transforming the opaque walls back into clear windows. "Jason?"

He forced his attention front and hoped like hell the CEO wasn't about to ask what the last slide was about. "Yes?"

"Let me be the first to officially congratulate you on your wedding. On behalf of everyone here at Maddox Communications, we wish you and Lauren a long and happy life together." Brock started a round of applause.

As the cheers and clapping subsided, Flynn stood. "Everyone here at Madd Comm is looking forward to getting to know your new bride better at the company dinner party."

"Absolutely, we'll be there." The dinner gathering would be more formal than their get-togethers at Rosa Lounge. Wives were expected to attend. Rumor had it that Flynn's estranged wife had chaffed under all the pressure that came from the hours demanded by MC to stay ahead of Golden Gate Promotions.

Jason cricked his neck from side to side, not sure how anyone managed to balance it all, especially in today's competitive market where there were plenty of hungry dogs ready to take his portion. Success had an added edge for him now that he had a wife and baby depending on him.

Gavin clapped him on the shoulder. "What the hell are you doing here leaving that pretty new bride of yours alone?"

"Don't be eyeing my accounts while I'm away," Jason answered, only half joking.

"Wouldn't dream of it," Gavin said, his own competitiveness shining through. But that edge would keep MC on top, which was good for both of them.

Jason rolled his large leather chair back, his feet itching to hit the road. He couldn't afford to take his eye off the ball at work, but an afternoon away the day after his wedding seemed more than reasonable. In fact, it would look strange otherwise. And he did need to make inroads with Lauren to keep her and the baby in San Francisco. "I'm knocking off early today. Lauren and I are planning our honeymoon for later. She understands I have the Prentice account to contend with right now. In fact, she's looking forward to meeting Walter Prentice at the big bash."

Brock studied him through narrowed eyes, assessing. "Perhaps we'll have a chance to get to know your bride in a more informal setting, maybe for an after-work drink at Rosa Lounge sometime this week."

"I'll speak with Lauren and let you know."

Brock nodded shortly. "Sounds like you have a real keeper there, sharp business lady, to boot."

"Thank you. Lauren's a special lady. I'm happy she's willing to follow me out here to California, especially given she has a company of her own back East." There. He'd laid the groundwork for her returning to New York as he'd promised her he would do, but damned if he would give her up that easily.

Her?

It was about their baby, right? About being a full-time father to his kid in a way his father had never been for him and his sister. Hell, time to stop lying to himself. He wanted Lauren here. He wanted her in his bed and in his life. She fit. They'd already proved they got along well as friends and at work.

They definitely were in synch sexually.

California was the right place for her to stay. He could ease the stress for her at work and in her family. They could have it all here in San Francisco. He just had to convince Lauren.

Now that he thought about it, she knew as well as he did that they had chemistry. He'd put all his effort into seducing her when he should work on convincing her on a practical level, showing her the ways their lives could fit together. He needed to think less about returning to his wife's bed and more about persuading her they could make a real family here together in San Francisco.

So for now, he would keep his hands to himself while he romanced his wife.

Lauren tugged her bathrobe tie tighter as her foot hit the last step leading into the hall. Supper with Jason had left her edgy, the carry-in Latin cuisine amazing, their legs brushing against each other at the kitchen island frustrating. She'd hoped a shower would help ease the tension, but no luck. She'd spent the whole time under the spray imagining inviting him to sit on the seat opposite her.

Then joining him to straddle his lap, instead.

A trickle of water slipped from her hair down the V of the robe, between her breasts, heavy and achy with desire. She stared through the carved archway into the living room. A fire crackled in the fireplace. Jason knelt in front, jabbing at the logs with a poker. Jeans pulled taut across his lean hips, the muscles in his thighs rippling against the faded denim and calling to her fingers to explore his strength up close and personal. The blaze in the hearth and between her legs both beckoned. She walked closer, the wood floor chilly beneath her bare feet.

His back still to her, Jason stood. He reached into a cardboard packing box and pulled out a thick striped comforter. With a snap of his wrists, he whipped the spread out and let it rest on the floor in front of the crackling fire.

"Did you finally give up on the chair and opt for the floor?"

He smiled back over his shoulder. "You seemed pretty awake at supper, so I thought you might want to hang out and talk."

"Talk. You want to talk?"

"Sure. Why not?"

Thinking of her sailboat drawing he'd kept framed in his home office gave her the courage to step into the romantic setup he'd prepared. On the corner rested the same black lacquer tray he'd used to bring her breakfast. A couple of cooking utensils—grill tools?—rested on the edge. This time, the wineglasses contained...

"Grape juice. I thought it was only fair you enjoy grapes in some form, since you have to bypass California's amazing wines for a few more months."

Tucking her robe around her knees, she sank onto the comforter. "How was work? Was everyone grilling you for details about the Vegas nuptials?"

"Some natural curiosity. Lots of congratulations." He glanced over his shoulder quickly, then went back to work on the fire. "Everyone wants to get to know you better, of course. There's a dinner party this weekend for the big Prentice account."

"Of course I'll be there. That's why we did this whole marriage thing, right?"

He jabbed the fire, his pause overlong. "The office also goes to a local hangout for drinks every now and again. We don't have to go this week if it's too much for you. You're working all day, as well."

"Drinks are fine—well, water with lime—but I don't have a problem spending time with the people from MC." Except for Celia. That could be damn awkward now that she thought about it. Suddenly she didn't want to talk about work anymore. "You have a way of making the no-furniture thing work...well, other than your furnished office upstairs." She glanced out the corner of her eye, watching for any telling reaction from him.

"I brought a few things from New York with me." He nodded toward the packing boxes. "Linens. Kitchen supplies. My clothes and some books."

"And your computer desk?" And the sailboat she'd drawn.

"Sure." He pressed a hand to the plush comforter. "This was my bedspread back in New York."

"For freezing winters, but not milder San Francisco temperatures, so it's stayed in the box so far." How strange to lead an unpack-as-you-go kind of existence.

"Exactly. Not so cold here."

"But chilly enough for a fire tonight." She angled forward to inhale the rich woodsy scent of an authentic fire. No gas logs here.

"And warm enough for gardens." He rolled up his shirtsleeves as the temperature in the room rose. "I was wondering if you would take a look at the flower beds and offer some suggestions."

A full-out plan already grew through her mind like vines clinging to a trellis, much like the one she could envision in his backyard leading to a hot tub. But this wasn't her house. She wouldn't be staying, and right now she wasn't sure she could take having more things to regret leaving behind when she returned to New York. "Wouldn't you rather hire a landscaper?"

"I would rather have my highly talented graphic-artist wife draw up a plan and put the landscaper to work. But only if you have the time, of course." He dipped his head into her line of sight. "I mean it. I'm not BSing you here."

She would probably regret this later, but... "Okay then, I'll take a look and sketch some ideas." She stared at her wedding rings. "It'll be fun thinking of things the baby will enjoy when we come to visit."

"Great," he said, smiling—another thing she would miss seeing when she left. "And speaking of the baby, I brought late-night snacks to go with the grape juice, if you're hungry." He reached behind the packing box and lifted a small grocery sack.

"I'm always hungry at the end of the day now." The baby fluttered inside her as if already anticipating whatever he had inside that bag.

"I'm glad you're feeling better." He pulled out graham crackers, marshmallows...

...and Godiva chocolates.

Her mouth watered. She eyed all the ingredients in his hands. "We're making Godiva s'mores?"

"Unless you don't want them. I understand about

finicky cravings." He tucked the gold box against his chest. "I can eat them myself."

"Do it and die." She snatched the box of chocolates, tore off the ribbon and popped one of the truffles in her mouth. "Mmm."

His smile went downright wicked. "I take that to mean you do want a s'more."

"Or three," she said, relaxing into the makeshift camp. Although they hadn't stocked Godivas in the tent when she'd been a Girl Scout.

She sat cross-legged on the thick comforter, leaning back on a packing box, the fire warming her as much as the romanticism. Jason put together the s'more and rested it on a grilling spatula with efficient hands. The way he read just what she needed touched a part of her she hadn't known sought tending. She prided herself on her independence, her competence. And while she could have fed herself, she never would have come up with Godiva s'mores.

While she may have known Jason for a year already, he was still surprising her more and more by the second. Like how well he'd handled the discussion on the plane about her mother's mental-health issues. "Thank you again for everything."

He glanced back over his shoulder. "Wait until you taste it first."

"I meant thank you for how understanding you were about my mother."

"I'm sorry she upset you on the phone." Firelight illuminated the genuine concern in his brown eyes. "I wish there was something I could do."

"It's okay. I don't really need her approval anymore."

"But she still has the power to hurt you," he observed too damn astutely.

"I guess maybe there's a part of us that never gets past wanting to see our artwork on Mom's refrigerator. The problem is, my mother only wants me to paint *her* kind of pictures. Her dreams." A dry laugh slipped free. "Although she certainly can dream big."

"Big is good." He placed the heated s'more on a small plate, chocolate and marshmallow oozing from the sides, and passed it to her.

"No. I mean big. Mount Everest big." She smiled her thanks and took the plate. "My mother had those grandiose kinds of fantasies. Two days into my tap lessons she was making plans for Broadway. A dive into the pool and she was talking Olympics."

"That's a lot of pressure for a kid."

"She had the same sort of plans for herself and her artwork. She always talked about how marrying Dad—" she dipped her finger into the warm, soft goo seeping from the treat "—and having me cost her Paris."

"Your mother is an artist?"

"An amazing talent, but the high-brow kind, which means she thinks I'm a sellout."

She popped her finger in her mouth and sucked off the chocolate-marshmallow mix just a smidge purposefully, enjoying the way he reached to loosen the neck of his shirt—only to find the top two buttons already undone. She couldn't deny the rush of pleasure, even the slightly hopeful edge after the torment of showering alone.

"You're a sharp businesswoman." His eyes tracked her every move, eyes turning as dark as the charred wood.

She couldn't help but revel in the appreciation in his

gaze. What pregnant woman wouldn't be happy to feel desirable and sexy? "So sharp my bookkeeper is enjoying all my profits on some island retreat."

She took a bite of her s'more, her tongue chasing every drizzle. Was that moan from her or from Jason?

"Crap like that happens. You're recovering." He shifted on the blanket, adjusting his jeans covertly. Well, almost covertly, except she couldn't miss the growing bulge pressing at his fly. An answering heat flamed inside her.

At least until her thoughts went back to her mom.

"I just question myself at times like this, examine every move I made for mistakes, carelessness. Lack of focus." She set her s'more back on the plate. The fun of the evening faded. "What about your parents? Have you called them yet?"

"I don't speak to my folks." He turned back to the grocery sack, preparing a second graham-cracker treat for the fire.

"That's sad."

"Why would you think that's sad? Wouldn't you be glad to dodge those judgmental confrontations with your mom?"

As much as her mother frustrated her, even hurt her sometimes, she couldn't imagine cutting her mom completely out of her life. What had driven such a wedge between Jason and his family?

"She's still my mother." Although she had to admit the extra distance between them California provided eased some of the pressure.

"You're mighty forgiving—except when it comes to me, of course."

Thinking back to her scene in his office, she winced.

"I thought you said you hadn't done anything wrong with Celia."

"I was talking about the way I handled the whole after-sex issue four months ago." He shoved aside the cooking gear and moved closer to her. "I should have missed the damn flight and stayed to talk to you."

"I told you to leave."

He stroked back her hair, his knuckles leaving a tingling path on her cheek. "And I should have asked if you meant it."

"At the time, yes." She'd been terrified of how out of control she'd felt in his arms, so much so she'd shown him the door as fast as she could. She'd thought at the time he felt the same way.

How they'd both only been able to let down barriers with each other when they had the assurance he would be leaving.

"What about now, Lauren?"

No chance of booting him out of her life again. "We're connected forever through the baby."

The air between them grew thick, the scent of him and the fire, the intimacy of the conversation all too much. She craved air. Now.

Arching back, she reached into the pocket of her robe and pulled out a copy of the ultrasound image. "I brought something to show you."

His eyes went wide, awe wide, as he glanced back up at her, then down at the picture again. "That's our baby?"

She nodded, determined not to let tears clog her throat. She could win this one battle over her damn hormones. The miracle of seeing the ultrasound for the first time washed over her again.

His thumb worked along the edge. "Do you know if it's a boy or girl?"

"They couldn't tell. The baby played shy, but the doctor said if they do an ultrasound later, they can look again. Do you want to know?"

"I'm fine either way." He looked her in the eye, his full attention a heady aphrodisiac. "I just need to know that you're both healthy."

His hand slid along her waist, rubbing the small of her back, soothing the ever-present ache, his touch and thoughtfulness stirring another ache altogether. Fire kindling inside her, spreading, she rocked forward. Everything he said and did tonight made her question her decision to stay in New York, made her want to throw away all she'd worked for just for a chance with him....

She snapped upright again and scavenged for the tattered remnants of her control. "The baby and I are both fine. There's nothing for you to worry about." Snatching up her s'more, she shot to her feet. "Thanks again for the dessert and the picnic, but I need to go to sleep."

He let her go with a low laugh that followed her all the way up the stairs. Damn him for being absolutely perfect tonight, enticing her with visions of what they could have together if she stayed in San Francisco. She stomped up the last two steps, not that it helped release the tension coiled inside her.

There was only one way to work that out of her system. She just didn't know if she was brave enough to risk taking it—*taking Jason.*

# Eight

Rosa Lounge wasn't at all what she anticipated.

She'd known ahead of time it was a martini bar, but she'd expected something along the line of New York high brow. Instead, she'd walked into San Francisco retro funk.

Loud music reverberated.

Pink lighting cast a hazy glow.

Black and white accents added a crisp edge.

The artist in her lapped up the visual contrasts.

And the food was to die for. She dipped an oozing grilled-cheese triangle into a cup of tomato soup. Her nausea a thing of the past, it seemed her appetite was making up for lost time. She nibbled a bite. Ah-mazing. Still, nothing beat Godiva s'mores with Jason.

Nothing about this time in San Francisco was turning out the way she expected. Did she dare risk more surprises by launching into an affair with Jason? The thought felt big and scary, so damn silly, really, when she already carried his baby. But there it was and she didn't know how to get past the hurdle to take what she wanted.

A light hand on her shoulder pulled her out of her reverie. Lauren turned quickly. "Yes?"

"Hello, we didn't get to speak earlier." A slim woman with dark brown hair clamped back unpretentiously thrust out her hand. "I'm Elle Linton, Brock's assistant."

"Lauren Presley...uh, Reagert. I'm still getting used to the new name."

"Of course." Elle smiled with understanding. "Elopements give you a little less time to get used to the changes coming up."

An elopement that came about in a very public and embarrassing fashion, thanks to her anger. Lauren looked across the bar and sure enough, Celia still stayed well clear of her on the other side at one of the tall tables.

Lauren turned back to Brock's assistant. "Jason and I have known each other for over a year."

"I'm sorry if my comments came out wrong. I didn't mean to sound nosy or imply anything." Her blue eyes lit with sincerity—and curiosity. This woman had a knack for getting people to spill their guts. "We're all just wondering about the lady who managed to land Jason Reagert."

Anger pulsed anew in time with the thrum of the music. "You mean since Celia Taylor was hitting on him just a few days ago?"

"Wow, Lauren—" Elle's eyes blinked wide "—you really know how to lay it all out there."

"Unless I'm mistaken, you all had a front-row seat to the scene in the office. I was a bit histrionic, I know." She winced at even describing herself that way, but God, she wanted out of this with her pride intact. And while creating a plausible cover story for Jason, damn his handsome ass. "I guess I just go a little catty when it comes to my man."

Ick. Had she really said that? And even worse, it was true. Her eyes gravitated to Celia again. The too-gorgeous redhead smiled tightly at the guy hitting on her, then eyed the door. She clearly didn't want to be here but couldn't seem to figure out how to leave. She had an outward confidence, but her agitation didn't quite match the way Elle had portrayed her.

"Lauren—" Elle rested her hand on her arm, angling sideways to let a waiter pass with a tray balanced on one hand "—nobody blames you for getting pissed. Celia's gorgeous and more than one person around here has wondered if she tried to sleep her way to the top."

Lauren hated the twinge of sympathy she felt for Celia. She knew how tough it was to get ahead in the business world without those sorts of rumors flying around. "That's pretty harsh."

Elle sipped her martini, eyeing her over the rim. "Unless it's true. I'm only saying, this is a very competitive crowd. Be careful."

Lauren watched Elle and found the woman's gaze skipped over to her boss, lingering. Could the assistant have some jealousy issues of her own? Regardless, Elle had a point. Lauren needed to step warily, especially around Brock's right-hand person.

And especially when she had a big fat secret of her own to hide in the form of a *fake* marriage. "Thank you for the heads-up, Elle. I appreciate your looking out for me and I'm sure Jason will, too."

"No problem. Just call me the troubleshooter."

Jason slid up behind her. "Hello, ladies. Can I get you refills?"

Lauren could smell his warm aftershave mixed with something distinctively him before he even announced himself. "I'm good, thank you."

"Me, too." Elle lifted her green martini in toast.

His arms slid around her as he stood against her back. "Everyone having fun?"

Lauren glanced up at him. "Just getting the lowdown on everyone at MC from the lady in the know."

Jason smiled. "That would be Elle."

Brock's assistant laughed dismissively, then eyed Lauren's sandwich. "I'm going to order one of those for myself. Nice talking with you."

Once the woman left, Lauren turned in Jason's arms, careful to balance her plate of food. "I think this is going well."

"Beyond well. You've more than done your bit for the evening. How about we relax?" He plucked her plate from her hands and set it on a nearby table. "Want to sit and eat, or dance?"

She almost blurted out a vote for her food, but then the heat of Jason's hands on her waist stirred a deeper hunger. More than anything, she wanted to be in his arms. What better way to test the waters on whether or not to pursue her sensual longings than to take to the public safety of the dance floor?

After all, what could happen there?

Three gyrating songs later, Jason pulled Lauren into his arms as a slow song came over the loudspeaker. She stiffened almost imperceptibly before sighing against him, a light sheen of perspiration adding an extra glow to her skin. The musky scent reminded him too quickly of sex. Of course, that tended to be a common thought for him whenever he saw Lauren, much less pulled her close.

She was temptation personified.

The dance made for the perfect chance to move forward with his plan to persuade her while holding back a while longer. He wanted her in his bed with no regrets this time.

He rested his forehead against hers. "Thank you for being so great this evening."

"Just holding up my end of the bargain." Her legs brushed lightly against his, her breasts pressed to his chest.

Okay, so maybe this hadn't been the brightest of ideas, after all. But hey, in for a penny—

"You really are amazing, and not just in a work setting. Do you know that?" He angled to skim his mouth against hers. Holding. Not so long as to make a sideshow event of things, but long enough for her to soften against him as he grew hard against her. Her lips tasted like a sweet ripe cheese and the lime from her water. And he didn't want to stop.

A couple jostled them and he eased his head away with more than a little regret.

Lauren looked up at him through thick eyelashes. "Are you trying to seduce me?"

Her voice came out husky and sexy, her chest rising and falling faster against him.

He slid his hands low along her waist, his finger aching for a more thorough exploration. "I only kissed you."

"You call that only a kiss?"

Her words revved the adrenaline zinging through him. "I do believe you complimented me."

She swatted his chest lightly, her cheeks a pretty pink. "You know full well what you were doing, what that was doing to me."

"You liked the kiss." He nestled her closer.

"Again, obvious." She swayed against him. "My body turns traitor when it comes to you. So *are* you trying to seduce me?"

Too obvious would lose the day here. He needed a more subtle, more romantic approach. "Who said a kiss has to lead to bed?"

She blinked back at him, surprise stunning her quiet.

"What?" He tucked her away from the crowded floor toward the outer edges, away from the speakers. "You disagree?"

Lauren shook her head quickly. "I don't disagree at all. I just didn't expect to hear something like that from you. From a man."

"I can assure you I am most definitely a man."

"I know." She rocked her hips lightly against his erection pressed undeniably against her soft stomach.

"Kissing you—" he brushed his mouth against hers lightly with promise "—brings me much pleasure."

And torment. But he didn't want to lose precious ground here by mentioning that.

MC's CFO—Ash—strode past on his way to dance

with his longtime girlfriend, a local law student. Did Ash remember that not more than three weeks ago right here at Rosa Lounge, they'd both declared themselves confirmed bachelors? Of course, Ash already had a failed marriage behind him.

Jason thumbed his wedding ring, reminding himself of the importance of patience. Keeping Lauren here in San Francisco required finesse. They'd already gone the route of jumping each other's bones at warp speed and that had not ended well for him.

He did not repeat mistakes.

The band cranked up the pace and Jason linked fingers with Lauren, leading her away from the increasingly packed space. He ducked closer to her ear. "Want to drive up to Twin Peaks for a romantic view of the city, perfect place to make out? I promise not to take advantage of you on our first date."

She snorted a laugh. "It may have escaped your notice, but we've already had sex."

"Believe me, I noticed." And remembered. And wanted more. Which meant sticking to his plan. "I take it that's a no to making out. Damn shame."

Her eyebrows pinched together in confusion. "Jason, I don't understand you tonight. I'm not sure what you expect or want—"

"Shh." He pressed a finger to her lips. "And by the way, nobody asked you for sex tonight. I'm an ad man, remember? You need to pay close attention to my words."

He stepped back and kissed her hand before letting go. "Thank you for a most enjoyable dance, Mrs. Reagert. I'll think about you all night long…while I'm sleeping in my chair."

\* \* \*

Two restless nights later, Lauren mingled at the MC dinner party. As unsettled as she was in her personal life, this business party did remind her of all the things she enjoyed about her job, the wheeling and dealing, the exchange of ideas with the best in the industry. She thrived on it.

Of course, that provided a whole new layer to her frustration.

Because this party also reminded her of all the reasons she wanted and needed to go back to her business in New York City, especially when her body screamed even more loudly for satisfaction with Jason. He was tormenting the hell out of her with his "accidental touches" and surprise kisses at every turn. Her skin felt on fire.

The live band segued from the swing music they'd played during dinner to classic rock. She wasn't sure she could hold out through another dance with Jason. Except it wasn't just on the dance floor where they were so in synch. In the upheaval of the past few months, she'd almost forgotten what an awesome team she and Jason made professionally. Tonight's gathering brought that all back to her.

Swaying to the beat, she nodded her thanks to the congratulations zinging from all sides as she made her way to the bar for a refill on her water. For the first time this evening, she and Jason worked opposite sides of the room, dinner finished, the mingling and dancing just beginning to crank into full swing. She felt his eyes following her, though. Her copper satin dress swished around her legs, each brush teasing her already overloaded senses, the beaded top suddenly itchy and uncomfortable against her breasts. God, she so needed to get her mind in the moment and off the way Jason made her feel with just a look.

The dinner party—catered by Wolfgang Puck's local Postrio—was being held in an exclusive yacht club that sported a fabulous view of San Francisco Bay. Through the wall of windows, she could see the Golden Gate Bridge through the mist.

It was one hell of an impressive party, from the five-star dinner to the A-list guests, everything running smoothly, thanks to Brock's ever-efficient assistant zipping to and fro.

Growing up in Connecticut, Lauren had wined and dined with influential families and major players in political circles. Even so, she was impressed. Maddox had pulled out all the stops.

With her nausea totally abated, her appetite had kicked into full gear. She could well enjoy everything from the crusted Alaskan halibut to the sweetheart plum dessert. Too bad she couldn't pack a doggy bag.

For another picnic in front of the fire? She shook off the memory.

The best of California wines flowed. Not that she'd been able to drink any, but the fragrant bouquets wafted through the room, mingling like the high-end guests. She sipped her sparkling water with lime.

"Mrs. Reagert," a voice called from behind her, "may I refill your drink?"

Lauren glanced over her shoulder to find the offer came not from a waiter but from Jason's big-catch client, Walter Prentice. Apparently even the ultrauptight client enjoyed a vintage wine on occasion.

"Thank you, Mr. Prentice. I was just making my way over."

"Then let me help you with that." He snapped his fingers impatiently and a waiter magically appeared to take her order, as well as a refill for Prentice's wife. The poor woman looked as if she could use a shot of something stronger to lift her spirits. Her husband was obviously devoted to her, but the worry lines across the woman's brow, the sad frown that didn't appear new hinted that Angela Prentice wasn't as happy as her husband.

Taking her fresh sparkling water from the waiter, Lauren smiled her thanks.

Prentice rocked back on his heels. "Sharp group of up-and-comers working with Maddox. It was a close competition between them and Golden Gate Promotions, but I'm pleased to be with such a dedicated and savvy group of young people."

Lauren glanced around the room at the major movers in the business. "I'm still getting to know everyone, but they've been wonderfully welcoming."

CFO Asher Williams placed his empty wineglass on a tray and led his law-student girlfriend onto the dance floor. Gavin Spencer shifted restlessly from foot to foot, the musclebound guy tugging at the neck of his tux absently as he listened intently to a cell-phone-company heiress.

Angela Prentice touched Lauren's arm lightly. "Tell me your name again, my dear."

"Lauren Presley, uh, Reagert now, of course." She smiled. "But the Presley part is no relation to the King."

Walter laughed full and loud. "I imagine you get asked that often."

"Often enough." She thought through what she knew

about Prentice and zeroed in on his company mantra. *Family Is Everything.* "Although my family is from Connecticut, nowhere near Graceland."

"Lovely country in Connecticut. I have a place on the coast." The billionaire probably had places on every coast. "You knew Jason in New York?"

"I own a graphic-arts business. We collaborated on a few accounts, and our relationship formed from there." True enough, even if the details might have sent Prentice into an apoplectic fit.

Angela pressed two fingers to her furrowed brow. "How will you manage your business from clear across country now that you and Jason are married?"

Prentice frowned. "I hope you don't intend to try one of those bicoastal relationships. They never work, you know. That's why I have my wife and children travel everywhere with me."

No wonder the woman had bags under her eyes.

"A lot can be accomplished with a good office manager, a computer and telecoms." She'd actually been thinking through some possibilities already, since making sure Jason was a part of their baby's life would require a great deal of travel on both their parts, especially for the next few years.

Which would also necessitate spending time together. A lot of time. Her eyes gravitated to Jason, speaking with Flynn, MC's vice president. The VP's broad shoulders and swagger drew more than a few female eyes in the room, but Lauren preferred Jason's lean swimmer's build. She could almost smell the salt air and sun on his skin.

Lauren yanked her focus back to Walter Prentice, who was speaking.

"You're a modern-day businesswoman."

She stiffened. Was that good or bad in his eyes?

Angela rested a gentle hand on her arm. "Congratulations again, dear, to you and Jason on the marriage and the baby. Walter and I are happy for you and your growing family."

"Hear, hear." Walter lifted his glass in a toast. "Now if you'll excuse us, Mrs. Reagert?"

"Of course. Nice speaking with you both." Lauren relaxed as the older couple walked away. Jason had read the situation right. All was well. She thumbed her wedding band, watching the Prentices. Forty years married. What would that be like? Staying with one person for more than half your life? While the Prentices seemed to have everything, Angela's sad eyes made Lauren think about all she had in New York.

Shaking her head, she pivoted and came face-to-face with…the very woman she'd been avoiding most of the evening.

Celia Taylor winced visibly.

Lauren considered making a quick excuse and speedy exit, then changed her mind. Running or evading would only fuel possible rumors. And weren't there already enough rumors about this woman floating around? While she should hate Celia, instead, she felt kind of sorry for her. The business world could be catty and vicious to beautiful women.

So Lauren plastered a big—hopefully genuine-looking—smile on her face. "Hello, Celia. I was just looking for you. I'm still new in town and was wondering if you could recommend a good hairstylist."

Sheesh, that sounded lame. So much for ignoring

the issue of looks. Why hadn't she thought to ask about work? Or consult on some other business matter? Or even ask for a freaking art gallery? Hell, she was committed to the conversation, so might as well forge ahead. She really wanted to smooth over any awkwardness with Jason's coworker.

Celia blinked fast, scrunching her too-darn-perfect nose. "Sure, sure, I'll e-mail you the name of my salon and spa."

"I appreciate it." She also needed to find a new ob/gyn out here, as well, if she was going to visit Jason again. Or maybe stay longer.

"I'm sorry about the other day," Celia said softly, leaning closer, her cologne expensive and probably delightful, but pregnancy heightened Lauren's sense of smell in a fickle way. It had to be the pregnancy, right? Not the fact that right now she resented the woman for merely existing.

Now wasn't that utterly ridiculous? Celia Taylor hadn't done anything wrong. The jealousy was totally Lauren's issue, not this woman's. "Really, there's no need for things to be awkward."

"Of course not. I just wanted to make sure you know there's nothing between Jason and me. I mean, I was asking about after-work plans...if he was going to Rosa Lounge with others from the office."

Celia wouldn't have asked in the first place if there'd been an inkling Jason was already in a relationship. Except he hadn't been. Not really. If their mutual friend hadn't sent Jason that photo showing Lauren pregnant, would he have accepted Celia's drink offer?

Jealousy nipped all the harder, after all. Reminding

herself it wasn't Celia's fault didn't seem to be helping. "Seriously, it's okay. I was the one who insisted on keeping our relationship quiet. If there's anyone to blame for it not being obvious Jason was already taken, the fault is mine."

Celia exhaled long and hard. "I'm so relieved to hear that. I hate office gossip. God, you're a really nice person."

Then why was she obsessing over how Celia didn't have to wear a tent of a dress to hide her stomach? No water retention on that woman, for sure.

And why was she thinking about impressing the Prentices? And finding an ob/gyn in San Francisco?

Because like it or not, she was drawn to Jason. For four months she'd been trying to work him out of her system—unsuccessfully. Ignoring him hadn't worked.

Lauren looked across the room again, finding him, wanting him. Jason's chin tipped as if he sensed her watching him, sensed *her*. He turned his head almost imperceptibly and his intense eyes locked with hers. A delicious tingle of awareness prickled over her, tightening her nerves with a deep need to wriggle against him skin to skin.

She couldn't run from the truth any longer. Her passion for Jason hadn't even begun to be tapped out. Denying it—denying herself—only made the ache grow stronger as pressure built.

She understood all about hormonal rushes from pregnancy, and maybe that added an edge, but still she knew it was something beyond just the raging hormones. She certainly hadn't tried to jump any of the other men who crossed her path, and heaven knew there were plenty of hot, high-powered men in this room.

But she only wanted Jason.

Starting tonight, she would try a new approach. Indulging every fantasy she'd ever entertained about her brand-new husband.

# Nine

The MC dinner had been a success. Jason had everything he'd wanted.

So why was he so damn irritable?

Stuffing his hands in his tuxedo pockets after locking up the house for the night, he stared at his sexy wife on the other side of their living room, fairly certain she was the cause of his frustration. The ride home had been off somehow. He'd pointed out scenic spots of interest along the way, trying to show her the upside of living here, but she stayed silent for the most part, staring at him with an intensity he found unsettling, since he didn't have a clue what she was thinking.

Lauren stood in the bay window, moonlight streaming through and glinting off the metallic beads on the bodice of her evening gown. She was both stunning and elegant at once. She was perfect in every regard. So much so, she made *him* see just how well their lives could fit together.

This hands-off idea of his was growing old fast. He wanted it all—wanted her—now. Her dress showcased her generous breasts until his hands shook from restrained desire. Gathered high on her waist, the loose folds hid any evidence of the baby, satin fabric pooling around her feet in low heels. Her hair was smoothed into a sleek twist with one long strand grazing her cheek like the stroke of the backs of his fingers along her jaw.

Male eyes had followed her all night long, damn near making him crazy with the need to remind them she was with him. She carried *his* baby. But he wouldn't behave like some kind of possessive ass.

Besides, he was too proud of her. He'd almost forgotten what a savvy businesswoman she was. She'd won over not only Prentice, but had worked the room, charming people and making contacts that would help her, as well as him. What a surprise to find her serene confidence turned him on just as much as her lush curves.

He stopped behind her, cupping her bare shoulders, determined to help her see how well their worlds were in synch. "You were amazing tonight. You absolutely had Prentice eating out of the palm of your hand."

She looked back, the lone strand of hair caressing her face the way he longed to do. "He seems a nice enough man, nicer than I expected, actually, after how rigid he seems in his criteria for how other people should live their lives."

"He certainly took to you." Jason slid his arms around her, encouraged that she didn't protest or stiffen. He linked his fingers over her stomach. The baby rolled lightly, then settled. "His wife did, too, for that matter."

"She seems like such a sad lady." Lauren leaned back against him, the sweet scent of her shampoo seeping deeper inside him. "I can't help wondering if the high-powered lifestyle suits her as much as it does him."

"How about you? Do you enjoy that kind of gig?" An important part of his life that could cause a real problem. The MC work-grind-and-party circuit had certainly tanked Flynn Maddox's marriage.

"Are you kidding? You've known me for a year. I thrive on that sort of wheeling and dealing." She shifted to fit more firmly against him, her bottom nestling intimately until there was no damn way she could miss his throbbing response.

"You certainly keep your cool under pressure." His blood pressure, however, was skyrocketing over just the feel of her brushing back against him. Right now he just wanted to sink into the moment. With her.

She glanced at him. "What are you thinking?"

Might as well be honest. "Just can't look away from you. You're absolutely gorgeous."

"Stop. You don't have to flatter me." Her hands slid over his on her stomach. "I know my waist disappeared a couple of weeks ago."

"I wasn't the only one who noticed you." Primitive possessiveness pumped through him all over again. "You're sexy as hell. That pregnancy-glow stuff is for real." His wayward thumbs brushed the undersides of her breasts. "All week long I've been aching to touch you."

She laughed lightly, turning in his arms to face him,

giving him a clear view of creamy cleavage. "Ah, so it's all about the extra cup size."

"An extra cup?" Hell, call him Cro-Magnon, but he absolutely couldn't tear his eyes off her chest, couldn't stop the thoughts of how much he wanted to peel her clothes from her and see every inch he'd missed during their hurried, half-clothed, one-time coupling. "Do you know what I'd give to see you out of that dress? God, Lauren, I heard what you said about no sex, but I'm about to die from wanting you. I don't know how much longer I can keep my hands off you."

She toyed with his tie, her fingers soft and enticing against his neck. "Maybe I've revised my thinking on the no-sex notion."

Her words slammed through him. He'd been hoping to make progress with Lauren, but could the dinner have shown her the same practical synchronicity of their lives that he'd observed?

Regardless, he certainly wasn't going to question the awesome opportunity of having her warm and willing in his arms.

Jason brushed a kiss along her ear, nuzzling aside the loose strand of hair. "*Maybe* revising your no-sex policy?"

She turned to meet his mouth, her body fluid against him, her arms sliding up around his neck. Her pupils widened with desire, urging him on. "*Definitely* revising."

Growling his relief, he kissed her, finally and fully, finding her open and ready and boldly seeking. It had been too long, too many nights waking up hard and unfulfilled from dreaming about her.

Lauren clutched at his shoulders, her hands strong

and insistent, like a woman who knew exactly what she wanted. Her fingers crawled up his collar and furrowed into his hair, urging him closer. Not close enough, since they still wore too damn many clothes.

He cupped her bottom, bringing her flush against him—which reminded him of his need for restraint. "What's the best way to make this happen that's safe for you and the baby?"

With nimble fingers, she swept aside his tuxedo jacket. "At four and half months, it's really not an issue yet. The books and my doctor all say to get inventive with positions down the road. Perhaps we should start practicing ahead of time?"

"You're putting some mighty powerful images in my mind." Of her now...of her later. Would they still be together then? He had a chance to sway her and he intended to make the most of it, because he was quickly learning that just a taste of Lauren was nowhere near enough. "How is it that you can turn me inside out with just that sexy voice of yours?"

"Words can be an aphrodisiac, too. I have some fantasies I'd like to share."

With one hand, he reached past her and whipped the curtains closed. "Listening to you talk about anything beats the hell out of oysters any day of the week."

Sighing her agreement, she nipped his bottom lip. He tugged the zipper down her spine, the expensive gown parting, sliding free to reveal...

His mouth went dry.

Lauren stood in a strapless lace bra and tiny matching bikini panties that sketched just below the gentle curve of her stomach. Metallic gold threads glinted in the off-white lace, drawing his eyes to alluring curves and creamy skin. He touched, stroked, couldn't think of anything more gorgeous than Lauren swelling with his child. The woman was a walking fertility goddess. He went so hard he thought she could very well bring him to his knees.

Her eyes heavy lidded with undisguised excitement, she plucked pins from her hair and shook the sleek updo free in a tumble over her shoulders. "One of us is vastly overdressed. Ditch the clothes, wonderboy. I have definitely been fantasizing about having you pose for me naked."

"Pose?" His hand hesitated on his buttons.

"I took art classes in drawing the male body while in college, you know."

He frowned. "I'm not so sure I like the idea of nude guys hanging out with you."

She trailed a nail down his chest. "Then get naked."

"Happy to accommodate." His eyes locked on hers, he shrugged out of his shirt, toed off his shoes and socks. Urgency pulsed through him, but taking his time meant he got to stare at her all the longer. They'd gone at each other so fast in her office, there hadn't been a chance for him to memorize the look of her.

Although the feel of being buried deep inside her silken walls was seared in his mind.

He kicked aside his pants and boxers, and extended a hand for her. She clasped his hand in one of hers and with her other, scratched a manicured nail down his chest. His heartbeat surged in response.

He tugged her toward him and she leaned against his chest, giving him easy access to unhook her bra and sweep it away. Satin and lace glided over his hands before sailing to the floor.

She arched against him, flattening her generous breasts to his chest with a moan of pleasure. "I don't think I can wait any longer. Can we go slow the second time?"

"My pleasure." Because a second encounter meant she wasn't going to boot his ass out right away afterward.

He backed her against the wall, grateful for the blank space, not that he would have given a damn if they'd knocked a Monet to the floor. She kissed him, bit him, scored her finger down his back as she shared ideas for the two of them together—white-hot fantasies—that let him know loud and clear she burned for this as much as he did. He swept away her panties, allowing himself a leisurely second to feel her warmth still lingering on the scrap of fabric. Amazing, but no substitute for the real thing, which happened to be right here in his arms.

Lauren hooked a leg on his hip and he didn't need any further invitation to explore. He found her slick and ready. He dipped his head to her breasts, drawing a taut nipple between his teeth carefully. The sound of her sigh, the way she tightened in his mouth, sent a charge through him until he throbbed against her stomach.

She cupped him, stroked him, her intent clear.

"Now? Here? You're sure?" Even clearly seeing the passion in her eyes, the same wild want he'd found four months ago, he needed to hear her say it, to confirm she wanted frantic sex against a wall as much as he did.

Her grip tightened ever so slightly. "If you don't take the edge off, I'm going to explode without you in about ninety seconds."

He throbbed in her hand. "Ninety seconds?"

"Eighty-nine." She circled her thumb over him.

He hitched her other leg up until she locked her ankles around his waist. He cupped her behind and lifted, positioning... She braced her hands on his shoulders and lowered, taking him inside her again...the way he remembered, except better, because nothing could have felt this amazing.

Her head fell to rest on his shoulder.

"Everything all right?" he said against her hair, holding himself in check, barely. The room around them faded as his world narrowed to the silky warm clamp of her body.

"Seventy-one seconds," she gasped, "and counting." Her chest rising and falling rapidly, she rocked her hips. He didn't need any more encouragement than that.

He thrust while she wriggled to get closer. She whispered urgent pleas, her voice growing breathier, her skin flushing, and yes, he was watching every nuance of her face. They might be rushing, but he wasn't going to miss the opportunity to see her, a gift he'd lost out on their first time.

Now, he savored the graceful arch of her neck as she threw her head back. The perspiration dotting her brow, her eyes shutting tighter with each increasingly loud moan. The way she bit down on her lip until the cry of completion burst free in an awesome expression of just how high he'd taken her. Lauren's heels pressed deeper into his back, vise-gripping them together. Her voice ricocheted into the high ceilings, their coming together noisy and uninhibited in a way they hadn't been able to indulge in at her office.

Who'd have thought his reserved wife would be a screamer? And the knowledge that he'd been the one to bring those sweet cries from her mouth sent him slamming over the edge in explosive release.

His forehead resting against the wall, he slumped against her, her legs still wrapped around him. Sweat sealed them skin to skin, linking them together. But for how long?

Because in just ninety seconds, he'd realized he couldn't ever let her go.

God, she needed to run.

Lauren straddled Jason's lap as they sat on the wooden seat in the spa shower. Spray pelting her back, she kissed water from his shoulder while he throbbed inside her.

Aftershocks from her own completion still shuddered through her, her mind full of images of how he'd loved her through the night with his hands, his mouth, his body. Even his words as he told her over and over how much he wanted her, how hot she made him feel, how he couldn't wait to have her again. She'd been totally out of control.

And that scared her to her dripping-wet toes.

Her skin cooling in the aftermath, she still couldn't bring herself to move off his lap.

She'd remembered sex between them being good, but this tangled, combustible passion they'd explored again and again was beyond good. It was reckless and messy and mind-numbing, so much so that she could lose reason altogether and forget the independent life she'd painstakingly built for herself. She'd worked so hard to break free of the smothering, constricting family life she'd grown up in. Would she have the strength to assert herself with Jason when he could so quickly reduce her to a puddle of pleasure?

When they'd stepped into the spa shower together, she'd been sure she couldn't make love again so soon, but he'd vowed they could make their way through one more of her fantasies before morning. All too quickly the stroke of his hands over her lathered body had sent her spiraling again until their oh-so-vocal coming together had echoed around the tiled walls.

Slowly, intensely. This was different from their frantic coupling on her work sofa, where he'd left her too quickly. She'd ached for more.

Now? He wrung every last orgasm from her, taking her to new heights after an already sensual night of lovemaking. She was so damn scared. She shivered against him.

Jason kissed her ear. "You're cold. Let me take care of that for you."

He lifted her off his lap gently, settling her on the other seat across from him before turning off the shower, brass fixtures steamed over. He stepped out onto the plush bath mat, opened the warmer drawer and passed her an oversize towel.

"Thank you." She didn't bother explaining that her shiver had come from another source altogether.

Lauren wrapped the heated folds around her and moved closer to the small fireplace in the bathroom. While this one had gas logs, instead of real wood, still it crackled with warm decadence. She'd been blessed to grow up in an affluent home, but even so, this remodeled bathroom impressed her.

That poor couple who'd broken up while decorating

this home sure had put a lot of time and care into their renovations. Had they gotten a chance to enjoy the place at all before their marriage fell apart?

Toweling his back dry, Jason leaned to kiss her, firmly, but briefly. "Would love to linger, but I'm late for work."

"Just blame me and my darn fantasies." She forced herself to smile and go along with his lighthearted mood.

The faster she could get him out the door, the sooner she could restore order to her jumbled emotions. She could barely think now, much less trust herself to be reasonable.

All but impossible to do while watching his lean, muscled body saunter away into the walk-in closet. She recalled him explaining there had been a fifth bedroom on this floor, but a wall had been knocked out to create the spacious master bath and walk-in. How much daring it must have taken to boldly whack out walls, making such an irrevocable change in the hope that all would turn out the way you'd envisioned—a reckless daring she was pretty damn sure she didn't possess.

Towel wrapped around her body, she combed through her hair as he rushed to dress.

He slipped into his loafers and snagged his briefcase on his way across the room toward her. "Sorry I have to work on Saturday, but I'll be home by six. I have plans for the evening, so don't bother with supper. I'll be thinking about you."

He kissed her again, longer this time, lingeringly—lovingly?—his tongue bold and possessive. The fresh taste of his mouthwash, the tangy scent of his aftershave, all sent her senses into overload. The man did know how to kiss and kiss well. And somehow the kiss meant all the more right now, because it obviously wasn't going to lead to sex. They were both wrung out and he had to leave for work. The tender attention he gave to her lips, the time to just connect, spoke of something somehow as intimate as when he'd been buried deep inside her.

Her eyelashes were just fluttering open as the door closed behind him on his way out.

She sank onto the edge of the whirlpool tub. Even if she found the resolve to return to New York, she would come back here for visits with the baby. He would have to travel East, too.

How could she be in the same room with him in the future and not want him? Want this. Want more and more. For how long? Surely a fire this hot had to burn out.

And if it didn't?

She'd had a front-row seat to the way her parents' high-intensity emotions had consumed each other. She would be damned if she would relive it in her own marriage.

# Ten

He was making headway. He could feel it as surely as the sting of salt spray off the Bay.

Jason slid his arm around Lauren's shoulders as they walked along the pier outside the yacht club where they'd consumed one helluva big dinner. He winced with guilt over making a pregnant woman wait an extra hour for supper.

Damn, he hated running late, but this afternoon he hadn't been able to avoid it. Prentice suddenly changed his mind about signing a teen pop star to endorse a line of beachwear. Not to mention Jason was juggling four other new accounts that needed settling in. At least they'd gotten to go out together on a Saturday night for an official date. And he intended to make the most of every minute to show her the many ways San Francisco living rocked.

How better to show her a number of sights at once than from...

"You have a boat?" Lauren exclaimed, her feet slowing along the dock. Waterfowl flapped overhead, local marshes rich and teeming with migrating birdlife during the winter months.

"Did I forget to mention that?"

"Uh, yeah, you did overlook it, because I'm sure I wouldn't have zoned out this." She swept her hand toward his Beneteau fifty-foot, performance/racing sailboat.

"I got a good deal on it from a guy whose business went belly-up. The custom-made boat had only just been delivered and in the water for a couple of months before he realized he would have to consolidate to avoid bankruptcy court."

"It's new, then?"

"Less than six months off the truck." Zipping up his windbreaker, Jason could already feel the lulling give-and-take of the deck beneath his feet. He hoped she wasn't the type to get seasick. It wasn't a deal breaker, but it sure would suck, given this was his only real form of recreation. "Would you like to go out for a spin?"

"Uh, sure. Why not?" She blinked at his surprise shift in the evening plans.

Did she have a problem with being impulsive? He wouldn't have thought that from the way they made love when and wherever the mood struck. On the way to supper, he'd had to pull off onto a deserted road or risk a wreck. She been frenetic and demanding and he'd enjoyed the hell out of every minute of it.

Come to think of it, that could have also played into why they were late for dinner.

He helped her aboard, nodding his thanks to the club employee who'd prepped the sails so he could head straight out with Lauren. So far, she seemed at ease on the boat. Her feet steady, she settled into a seat and tipped her face into the wind. The slap and ping of sails and lines soothed him after a tense day at work.

Lauren seemed content with silence—something he appreciated since most people he knew felt the need to fill up quiet spaces. He guided the boat out into the Bay. The moon overhead and lights along the shore showcased a top-notch view of the shopping at Fisherman's Wharf and historic Alcatraz.

After an hour of cruising, he set the anchor and joined her on the bow of the boat. The boat's running lights sparked off the crest of waves, the shoreline lit with nightlife.

Jason draped a blanket over her shoulders and sat behind her. "Are you cold?"

She shook her head against him. "I'm fine. Lots of layers, just like you instructed before we headed out." She burrowed more deeply into the quilted folds. "But leave the quilt. It's getting colder."

He pulled her closer, enjoying the feel of her body tucked against his even through the blanket. "Did you have a productive afternoon working?"

"Not particularly creative, but busy. I'm taking care of creditors since your infusion of cash came through." She rested her hand on his bent knee. "Thank you again. My company means a lot to me."

"No thanks necessary." And he meant it. "You're paying me back, remember?"

She chuckled. "At an absurdly low interest rate."

He hoped they could just write off that whole damn debt soon. He'd meant to help her, and now he hated the way she seemed hung up on not taking anything from him. With luck, the private detective he'd hired to hunt down her accountant would turn up something soon. If she got her money back, then she would have stability in her company, which afforded flexibility.

He knew there wasn't a chance in hell she would accept more money from him, but perhaps he could persuade her to keep the original loan for their kid, expand her business with a San Francisco base. Best for the baby, right?

And damn great for him.

She glanced back at him, wind whipping her long auburn ponytail over her face. "I'm glad you suggested this. I imagine it's no surprise I've been a little stressed out lately."

"The water has a calming effect." Waves lapped the side of the boat, fish plopping a few feet away. Lights from a couple of other crafts glittered in the distance, but no one close enough for him to see details in the night.

"You could live here. The boat has more furniture than your house."

He decided the time had come to press her for more. According to her preset deadline, he only had a week left before she returned to New York. "Maybe Sunday we can wander around Fisherman's Wharf, do some furniture shopping."

"Jason, you're pushing." She traced the outline of his kneecap, her eyes still set on the horizon. "What made you decide to get out of the Navy? Prentice mentioned something over dinner about you being a hero during a pirate incident. You went really quiet."

He tensed at her surprise charge into his past. Then decided to let her subject change go unnoted, since she hadn't left his arms. "I was just doing my job. I only mentioned it to Prentice because he has a nephew in the service."

"What happened?"

His Navy time seemed such a world away now, but it was a part of him, giving him a discipline, drive and focus his old man had always insisted he needed, but was never around to teach or model. Jason felt his baby roll lightly under his hands and vowed to do better, to be present. "It was a hostage situation off the coast of Malaysia. We were called in to help."

"We?"

"I was a dive officer attached to a SEAL team, working EOD."

"EOD?" she prodded.

"Explosive ordinance disposal."

She shuddered against him. "Sounds scary."

Scary? In the early days, but in later years, the shakes usually didn't set in until after a mission. "There were some tense times, sure, but you train hard, then go on autopilot for the mission."

"Your job must seem tame now."

"Just different. Sometimes I miss it, but for the most part I'm content with what I offered my country. I'm ready to move on. This is what I studied to do in college. It's what I've always wanted to do. I was just so determined to be different from my old man that I chased other dreams for a while before coming back to what's in my blood."

"You've certainly stepped well out of your dad's

shadow, here and back in New York, too. You're your own man."

He appreciated that she saw that. He'd sure as hell tried. "I took a Navy ROTC scholarship to college since my inheritance from my grandparents wouldn't come through until I was twenty-five. After I graduated, I owed years of service in return. I like to think I would have joined even if I hadn't needed the money."

"Your parents wouldn't pay for you to go to college?"

"Oh, they would have paid, but there were too many strings attached."

"Like what?"

"Go to my father's alma mater, join the family firm. I appreciate the advantages my family provided while I was growing up, but I couldn't be a spoiled trust-fund kid."

"You definitely proved yourself."

"It's an ongoing process." Lifelong, in fact. He thought about her mother who'd so devalued Lauren's art because it wasn't the same as hers. Maybe Lauren understood his problems with his parents better than he would have realized before. "Overall, I'm happy here, with the locale and the job."

"Given your obvious love of the water, San Francisco is a good fit for you, then, much more so than the cold northern winters back in New York."

"I've been diving since I was in elementary school. It's convenient having my boat here rather than losing time jetting to a vacation spot." He rested his chin on top of her head. "The sunken ships are fun to explore, and the coral reefs are amazing here. I'd like to take you after the baby's born."

"Jason—" she pinched the inside of his thigh lightly "—you're pushing again."

And she was so warm and beautiful in his arms, he decided to nudge her a little further. "We can't take this one day at a time forever. Eventually we have to make plans."

She turned in his arms, her face luminous in the moonlight. "You know what? I have a plan, a really great plan for how we should spend this night together."

Damn it all, he was serious here. He wanted her to see all the ways their lives fit together as perfectly as their bodies. The determined glint in her eye gave him only a second's warning before she tackled him back against the deck.

Lauren tugged the blanket over them. "I think we should climb underneath this quilt and see who can make the other scream with pleasure first."

Lauren planted her hands on the deck on either side of Jason's face and kissed him, letting her body and her passion have free rein. The stunned expression on his face gave her the advantage she needed. But he didn't lag behind for long. Growling low, he rolled her underneath him, the blanket tenting over them.

All his talk of the future had increased the panicked need to flee until she decided to act. To shut him up the best way possible.

She didn't want to talk. He should already know full well she had dreams, a business, a need to make her own way in the world. And yes, even a need to look out for her mother, who had no one else to care for her, nobody to make sure she didn't slide completely over the edge.

And, oh, God, it hurt to think about that. But those needs were all calling to her to return to New York.

Her time here with him was running out. She only had a week left to store up memories, and then she would have to set boundaries in place if they were to have any hope of peacefully bringing up their child.

Right now, she just wanted to feel, to savor the lean, long stretch of his body over hers, memorize the sound of his voice hoarse with desire for her.

The boat undulated gently beneath them, nature's waves mimicking the motion of their bodies rocking against each other. She tore at his clothes with frantic hands until he brushed them aside and worked his jeans open and her pants down to her ankles. She wrapped her fingers around the throbbing length of him, his open zipper rasping against the back of her hand as she guided him.

And then, yes, thank heavens, yes, he was inside her, moving, loving, angling his weight off her. The spicy scent of him mingled with the salt air and her own floral perfume until her senses went on overload.

She gripped his butt through denim and urged him harder, faster, needing to be closer than her swelling stomach would allow. His hand slipped between them and he touched her. Tormented her. Eased her and drew her tighter both at once as he worked her with his fingers and his thrusting body.

Already they were developing an instinctive rhythm of their own, an understanding of each other's needs that excited and scared her. How could something be so amazing and so discombobulating at the same time?

He made her yearn to do scandalous things, like make love out in the open on the deck of a boat.

He nipped at her ear, his face in her hair as he continued to coax her, rubbing tight circles, his callused skin heightening the sensation. "So, Lauren, who's gonna scream first?"

She pressed her knees against his hips, massaging him with gentle squeezes until he groaned in her ear. "I don't know," she gasped, "you tell me."

He loomed over her, his face taut with restraint. "I think we're gonna make this a simultaneous thing."

His confident promise of synchronized satisfaction sent her closer to the edge.

He captured her shout with his mouth and she could have sworn she took in his hoarse growl of fulfillment, as well. Pleasure flowed through her veins like a molten rainbow palate, melting every muscle and bone and nerve until she sagged back on the deck.

Dragging in air, he slumped beside her, hauling her against his chest wordlessly. He tucked the blanket more securely around them both before hooking his arms around and under her breasts.

Lights winked on the San Francisco shore, a world away from New York. Yet with each slap of the waves against the hull, she couldn't escape the fact that with every second that ticked away, she was growing weaker where Jason was concerned. He'd presented his campaign well in showing her how perfectly their lives could fit together.

As much as she embraced cool logic and calm in her world, with her heart pounding out of her chest right now, she just kept thinking about how he'd never once mentioned the possibility of love. And she couldn't escape the churning sense that she was falling irrevocably in love with Jason.

# Eleven

Jason loped belowdecks after double-checking that the boat was secure for the night. Having Lauren all to himself in a bed until morning was a pleasure he intended to make the most of.

If he could keep up with her. The woman was damned near insatiable.

He smiled.

Pushing open the door to the main sleeping quarters, he stopped short. The sheets were rumpled, but the bed was empty. Where the hell had she gone? It wasn't as if there were many options.

He pivoted back toward the galley kitchen and flicked on the light this time. Sure enough, Lauren sat curled in a corner of the sofa, her eyes red from unshed tears. Wearing one of his T-shirts and not much else, she hugged her knees to her chest.

"Lauren?" he asked warily. "Everything okay?"

She straightened quickly, her smile overbright. "Of course. Why wouldn't it be?" She smoothed the U.S. Navy shirt over her legs, the cotton faded and soft from years of washing. "I've just had amazing sex under the stars and I suspect I'm going to get more great sex before the night's played out."

That was a bet she would damn well win. Soon. But not yet. Especially not until he figured out what had upset her.

Jason sat beside her, not too close, though. Something about her tense shoulders shouted she would crumble if touched her. "You seem distracted. And call me a selfish bastard, but when I have a woman in my bed—when I have *you* in my bed—I want your complete and undivided attention."

"It's nothing." She tugged at the hem of the shirt with nervous fingers, so unlike his normally confident wife. "Really."

"You're obviously upset." He rested his hand on hers, stilling her nervous fidgeting. "Why can't you just tell me?"

She reached under her leg and pulled out her cell phone. "My mother called again."

Rolling her eyes with a dismissive bravado that didn't quite play out, she pitched the phone to the end of the sofa. A light dip of the boat sent the cell tumbling to the floor.

Her mother? Good God, it was after midnight here, which meant it was later than three in the morning in New York. What was her mother doing calling Lauren so late? Inconsiderate to her pregnant daughter, who could have already been asleep.

Then it hit him. Jacqueline must have been in one of

her manic moods. He didn't know much about bipolar disease—something he intended to rectify ASAP—but he figured tonight's call couldn't have been pleasant.

He couldn't change the past, but maybe he could lighten her present. "Well, hell, Lauren, you should have thumped from below and I would have come to your rescue."

A wobbly smile eased over her face. "Thanks, truly, but you can't yank the phone away from me forever."

"What did she say?"

"Nothing all that horrible, really. Her timing just sucks, is all." She leaned a little closer. A promising move. "She's wigging out over the baby news. The wedding was okay in her eyes—not the baby. Or rather not the whole having-to-get married thing."

He tugged a lock of her hair gently. "I thought you said you found that kind of view archaic."

Her mouth went tight. "She told me to make sure I get a good divorce settlement, and after she hung up, she texted me the number of her attorney."

He stayed silent for three caws of night birds outside to keep from saying exactly what he thought of Jacqueline's interference. It was all he could do not to pick up the cell phone and toss it into the Bay. "Not exactly a supportive call from Mama, huh?"

Her hands clenched into fists. "I know it sounds silly. It's not like we're planning to stay married or anything. I just resented the way she expected me to take you to the cleaners. She made me think of that half-million dollars and it felt so damn wrong." She thumped the cushions with a fist. "I should have stood strong, let the company go under if that's the way things had to be. I screwed up."

"Whoa, whoa, slow down a second." He cupped her shoulders and turned her to face him fully. He might have some issues of his own he would like to press with her, but no way in hell was he going to let Lauren doubt herself this way. Damn Jacqueline for cutting such a wide swath through this amazing woman's confidence. "Let's unpack these thoughts one at a time. First, the creep stole from you. That happens to the most competent, smart people in the business world all the time. Hell, even entire cities get ripped off. Second, we are attached through this baby, which means we have to work together and help each other. If my ass lands in the fire, I damn well expect you to come help me. Got it?" He tapped her chin. "Do you hear me?"

She nodded, her smile a little steadier this time. "I do hear you, and I have to admit I like what you're saying."

"And lastly—" this one was for his own satisfaction, as much as hers "—quit giving a crap what your mother thinks. I don't want her upsetting the mother of my kid."

Her hands cupped either side of his neck as she cocked her head. "That point's not quite as reasonable as the first two, you know."

Yeah, and he felt a bit like a hypocrite since he'd let his father's opinion matter for most of his life. "Maybe when it comes to you I'm not as reasonable as I would like to be." Wasn't that the understatement of the year? "Now come to bed."

Her smile was slow, sensuous and full out this time. "Are you seducing me?"

"God, woman—" he slid an arm around her shoulders, his knuckles skimming the side of her breast "—you have a one-track mind."

She nibbled along his jaw. "Are you inviting me to make out again?"

Was he? Truth be told, he wanted something more from her right now. "I'm asking you to sleep with me."

"Sure, sounds great." She yawned her agreement, her voice offhand, totally missing the significance of what he was trying to say.

She wasn't even looking at him. She was already walking toward the cabin, her head tucked under his chin.

He tried to tell himself it was his impatience kicking into overdrive. This was no big deal. Yet even as they slid under the covers and she tucked close against his chest, Jason could sense she was holding a part of herself back. Playing out fantasies was fine for her.

But after the way she'd been burned in the past, he was beginning to see that Lauren ran like hell from the messiness of real life.

Long after Jason drifted off to sleep, Lauren stared at the moon and stars playing around in the sky just beyond the portal. The gentle rocking of the boat would have lulled her to sleep on any other night, but now? Too much turmoil churned inside her.

Tugging the comforter more securely over them, she tucked her leg between his, tangled up in the sheets, and savored the warm, bristly weight against her. If only they could stay on this boat, maybe move a little farther out to sea where her cell phone wouldn't pick up a signal.

She didn't cry. She wouldn't let herself. These middle-of-the-night calls from her mother weren't anything new, and she should have expected it. After all, there had to be fall-out for not telling Jacqueline about the baby. She'd just hoped this time…

Squeezing her eyes shut, she mentally kicked herself for expecting too much from her mother. She should know better after all these years of ups and downs. How damn stupid to get emotionally wrecked because she wanted to pick out nursery decorations with her mom. To talk about baby names, even. Instead, she'd been given the name of a divorce lawyer.

She was fairly damn certain she wasn't going to name her kid Horace—after her mom's current favorite attorney.

Lauren tucked herself closer to Jason and his arm slid around her waist in his sleep. Sighing, she snuggled even nearer, taking some of the comfort she hadn't been able to let her guard down enough to accept earlier.

Keeping things light was much better in the long run—it meant her heart wouldn't be as broken when they had to say goodbye.

"Damn it, Jason, a subject is supposed to be still. You're making this so much more difficult than it has to be."

A valid point. But he didn't think he was cut out to be a nude model. Of course, given he was the subject *and* the canvas, staying motionless was a little tougher than normal.

His muscles twitched from the effort, almost impossible with Lauren watching and touching him. "Aren't you out of syrup yet?"

Lauren stood naked just outside the small shower belowdecks while he "posed" inside the aqua-tiled stall. Halfway through their Belgian waffle breakfast, she'd eyed the remains of their food with glee. The next thing he knew, she'd scavenged a basting brush from the galley kitchen and returned with a bowl of warmed syrup. When she pointed to the shower, he hadn't argued.

She waved the brush, a droplet of maple syrup landing on top of his foot. "Don't move or I'll stop."

"You're wicked."

"Just indulging in another fantasy."

"Have your way with me, then." He winked, imagining a lifetime spent exploring more fantasies together. "I'm all yours."

The bowl rested in the sink and she dipped the marinating brush in the rich brown liquid. She swirled the heated glaze over his heart, slowly along his pecs, circling tighter and tighter until she flicked his nipple. His heart kicked up, harder, faster. He pulsed hot and ready to flip her onto her back and plunge inside her. Her eyes, however, warned him again she would stop if he so much as flinched.

With a sweeping stroke, she trailed lower, the sugary scent coating the air. She traced his ribs, dipping lower again until his abs contracted. He bit his lip.

"Are you ticklish?"

Not that he would ever admit. "No. What are you painting, anyway?

"A big, powerful tree." Her teasing touch brushed closer to his sides with branchlike sweeps. That sure was one leafy tree. "I think you *are* ticklish. I think the big strong guy has a weakness, after all."

He held still through sheer force of will. "It's only a weakness if I let it affect me."

"Is that a dare?"

He simply arched an eyebrow. Then he saw the impish intent in her eyes and prepped himself to hold still. She moved. Stroked.

Lower.

Not tickling at all, but boldly painting a bristly path over the hardened head of him straining up his stomach. He slumped back against the tile wall and this time she didn't rag him about moving. Lauren smiled with womanly power, continuing down, coating him all the way to his base.

Her grin broadened before she knelt and took him in her mouth. At the slick glide of her tongue, he forgot how to think or form rational thoughts. Sensation swept over him as she suckled and laved away every last bit she'd so torturously applied. Her moan of appreciation echoed a deeper one rumbling up his chest. Need pounded through him until his blood turned as thick as the syrup in the bowl beside them.

The brush fell from her hand and clanked against the tile floor a second before her cool fingers cupped him, massaging. His jaw clamped closed, and he planted his palms flat against the stall wall to keep from falling to his knees. And he couldn't even blame the rocking of the boat under his feet. Much more of the dual torment and he would lose control—before he made sure she was every bit as turned on as he was.

Jason gripped her waist and drew her away from him with more than a little regret. Regret quickly dispersed as he saw her dilated pupils, the flush of arousal tinting her skin, all signs that being with him affected her on a deep and visceral level, a level he intended to take even deeper. He cranked on the shower and plunged them under the spray. Icy pellets needled along his oversensitized skin, then quickly warmed.

Fitting his mouth over hers, he tasted syrup and desire and heat, and he couldn't get enough of her. They were messy and sticky, but nothing with Lauren had ever been simple. And he did so enjoy showering with her afterward.

Maybe after they finished in here, he could wring a promise from her to stay longer…then longer…until they settled into a life together.

Water rolled down them in a syrupy whirlpool spiraling into the drain. He hooked her leg over his hip until he nudged the moist core of her. Lauren dug her heel into his butt, leaning against him for balance. She writhed against him harder, her need for release evident in her insistent wriggles and breathy moans echoing with the call of early-morning birds outside the portal.

"Stay, stay here in San Francisco." The command fell out ahead of his brain. Damn. He'd meant to wait until after.

Jason sealed his mouth to hers, determined to distract her. It was just one lame-ass little sentence, after all.

Lauren went still against him, water streaming from her sopping-wet hair.

"What did you say?" she whispered, water spiking her eyelashes.

"We can talk later." He splayed his hands over her shoulders, down to cup her slick breasts, hoping to distract her and cursing himself. He knew timing was everything in an ad presentation, and winning her over was the most important campaign of his life.

She angled back, water sealing them together for a

moment before giving way. "I heard what you said." Her face was wary and closed and offered little clue to her thoughts, but she'd sure as hell put a stop to getting busy. "I just don't understand why you're changing the rules."

"You're the one who rescinded the no-sex ban." He palmed her back, keeping his touch low-key while reconnecting. "And I don't know about you, but for me, what we've done together changes everything. I want more."

She nibbled her lower lip, uncertainty clouding her eyes as she stared back in the narrow space. Hope steamed through him and he guided her between his legs.

She slid her hand up to cradle his face, her expression sad. "Why? Why do you want more?"

Not the answer he'd been angling for, but she hadn't slammed the door in his face. He scavenged for arguments to change her mind and came up blank. He'd used his best ammo from the minute he'd stepped into her apartment a week ago. Still, there had to be something—

His BlackBerry chimed softly, rattling against the galley-kitchen counter. He let it play out. Seconds later it chimed again.

Lauren stepped away, snagging a towel from the hook and wrapping it around her. "Just answer it."

"No—" he clasped her elbow "—we're in the middle of something important. I want you and the baby with me. I'll pay the relocation costs to move your business here, anything I can do to make the transition easier for you, because bottom line, New York is just too far away for the life I want us to build in San Francisco." Frustration clawed up his throat as he searched for the right way to persuade her. "Damn it, Lauren, this is the logical thing to do."

As soon as he finished his tirade, he realized he

hadn't come close to hitting the right button with her, and he still didn't have a clue what the answer might be.

Was she just that stubborn? That proud? A dark sense of foreboding crept over him like ants coming out to feast on the sticky sweetness drying on his skin.

"We're not in the middle of anything anymore." She snatched up his BlackBerry and thrust it toward him.

Left with no choice, he took it from her with the intent of just turning the damn thing off. The e-mail address scrolling across stopped him cold.

The private investigator he'd hired to find Lauren's crooked accountant.

Jason clicked on the message.

Have located the subject, his Cayman account and other holdings of interest. Details are ready to turn over to police. Please advise how you wish to proceed.

Keeping the information from her wasn't an option, even if tossing it aside increased her chances of staying. His opportunity to win Lauren had passed.

Now that her business was secure and she didn't need his money, there was nothing holding her in San Francisco.

Lauren had no reason to stay. Jason didn't love her, and she had no reason to believe her too-logical lover ever would.

From Jason's car, she looked at the houses leading up the steep street to his home. Her home, too, even if only for another week. She'd initially promised to stick around for two weeks to help solidify the Prentice account, and she would keep her end of the bargain, even if she didn't need his money anymore.

After the message had come in on his BlackBerry, Jason had told her about hiring a private investigator, about finding her slimy old accountant and the missing money, now tucked away in a Cayman account. Authorities were on their way to pick up the bookkeeper, and his assets in a number of other countries had been frozen. It didn't matter if they could get to the Cayman account or not, or how sticky extradition might be; the crook had enough cash stashed in other places she would have her money returned in the end.

In a week she would return to her little apartment in New York, her icy winters and her business. Thanks to Jason and his private investigator, she had her old life back. Eventually she could repay Jason what she'd borrowed. She had everything she wanted.

So why did she feel so empty?

It was going to be a long and miserable final week in Jason's house. How had she ever thought she could simply play out her fantasies with him, then leave without a mark on her heart?

Jason sat silently beside her, driving the car, the scent of his freshly showered body riding the light gust of his car heater. The morning was chilly, but nowhere near as cold as the knot freezing up in her chest. She just wanted to get to her room, away from Jason and the temptation to ignore reason and throw her carefully planned life away to move in with a man who'd never even told her he loved her.

Love?

Yes, she loved him, a certainty that was settling more

deeply inside her. But the simple word still scared her down to her toenails. She'd seen what love did to her parents and she wanted no part of that. Apparently Jason was as cautious with his emotions as she was, since he'd never alluded to feeling something so complicated and inconvenient—and wonderful—for her. What if she took a chance and told him? Maybe once they got home, over supper in front of the fireplace she could take that risk on the outside chance...

Jason crested the hill leading to his place. Lauren squinted for a better view in the early-morning sun, and sure enough a sleek luxury car was parked directly in front of Jason's house. He cursed low and long beside her. Lauren sat up straighter and peered through the window. A man leaned against the car, a tall guy with jet-black hair. His face became clearer as they neared.

None other than Jason's boss, Brock Maddox, waited for them. The man wore a suit. Was he on his way to church or work? Either way, finding him waiting here couldn't be a good sign.

Jason pulled up behind Brock's car, parking on the road. "I'll meet you inside in a few minutes," he said to Lauren before sliding out of the vehicle. "Good morning, Brock. What can I do for you?"

Lauren closed the sedan door, curiosity holding her on the sidewalk as Jason approached Maddox. She would go inside shortly.

Straightening from the car, Brock jammed his hands into his pockets. "Prentice is not happy."

Jason frowned. "What are you talking about?"

"This fake marriage you two tried to pull off."

Lauren stiffened. She might be torn by her decision

to go back to New York, but in no way did she want to cost Jason his job. She stepped alongside him, sliding a shaking hand in the crook of his arm. "Who says it's not real?"

Brock looked back and forth between the two of them as if weighing the wisdom of including her in the conversation. He didn't seem interested in going inside, though, opting instead to hold this meeting outdoors. Maddox was one cool customer, distant and perhaps even a bit uncaring. Was that what Jason had to look forward to becoming?

She rubbed the goose bumps prickling her arms. At least the neighborhood was quiet and deserted for the most part, other than a Jaguar driving past, engine growling low. Four doors down a small family piled into a car, all dressed to the nines for church. A lump swelled in her throat.

Jason's face went taut with tension. "Anything you can say to me, you can say to Lauren."

They always had managed well when it came to the business arena. The bittersweet thought tugged at her aching heart.

"Okay, then." Brock nodded. "The financial world is a small community. Did you think your half-million-dollar transaction wouldn't be noticed? Let me see if I can put this together just right, given the rumors floating around from Wall Street all the way to key players at Golden Gate Promotions. Lauren's accountant ran off with her operating capital, also a half-million dollars."

Hearing how clearly Brock saw through their ruse sent a bolt of panic through Lauren. She glanced at Jason, but he still kept his face impassive, apparently much better at tamping down freaked-out feelings than she was. Lauren forced herself to listen carefully to Brock.

"I'm guessing you bailed Lauren out in exchange for a pretend marriage to keep Prentice from going off the deep end over the pregnancy."

Lauren searched for the right words to save Jason's career. How damned ironic that just as hers came back together, his fell apart. "Ours may not have had a more traditional romantic beginning, but things have changed between us."

Not that it was any business of his. How could Jason manage a work environment that was so claustrophobic? Hell, so downright nosy? She considered blurting out how much she loved Jason.

Brock glanced back at Jason. "So Lauren's staying?"

Jason hesitated a second too long. "She doesn't have plane reservations."

Brock cocked an eyebrow. "You'll have to come up with better than that. Hell, I already know the police are involved and they locked in—what?—an hour ago?"

"My wife and I share finances. Her business is my business. What's wrong with my investing in her company?"

"That's not the way Prentice is seeing things. He's not too hyped on trusting a guy who paid a woman to participate in a pretend marriage just to save an account."

She bristled, prepared to tell Brock off, but held back for Jason's sake. Besides, for once the gossips were right on the mark.

Jason's shoulders braced with military bearing. "How do you intend to proceed?"

"It's your account. You brought it in, so it's yours to

manage. I won't lie—we've never needed an account like Prentice more than now. Competitors—Athos Koteas in particular—are breathing down our neck."

"I understand that and want to do what's best for MC."

Brock glanced at Lauren, then back. "It's obvious how far you'll go, and while a part of me admires that, I also expect you to cover your ass better." He scrubbed a hand over his jaw. "I'm kicking myself for not figuring this out sooner."

Jason pinched the bridge of his nose. Lauren felt like a fool, a heartbroken fool who'd stupidly fallen in love with her relentlessly ambitious husband. Thank God she'd resisted the urge to blurt out her feelings for him.

Brock pulled out the keys to his car, jingling them in his hand. "That's all for now. I just wanted to give you a heads-up in person, offer you time to come up with some way to pull your ass out of the fire. Prentice has called a meeting for tomorrow afternoon. But I'll see you in my office first thing in the morning." He nodded quickly to Lauren before sliding back in his car, all business.

Jason didn't even look at her, his gaze fixed on Brock's receding car. "I guess that's it for us, then," he said. "You won't even need to wait until next week for that flight out."

It was what she wanted. What she'd planned from the start. Her eyes shot back to the family down the street, her gaze lingering on the dad buckling the baby into a car seat.

If she had everything she wanted, why did it hurt this much to watch that little family down the street drive off together?

# Twelve

The next morning Jason left Brock's office after a damage-control meeting to prep strategy for the Prentice powwow later today. His brain was too numb to do more than operate on autopilot to salvage what he could at work. He'd lost Lauren and would be relegated to parceled-out visits with his kid.

Last night he and Lauren had been back to sleeping separately, with him in the recliner and her in the bed. She'd made it clear it would best if he was gone before she woke up. She would keep in touch about the baby, but she didn't want any big emotional goodbyes.

He turned away from Brock's door. Brock had pretty much given him a speech to memorize, a pack of convoluted lies about how things had shaken down, but well-constructed lies Prentice might well buy into. His job was all that was left. A bigger office with a better window view was all he had to look forward to.

Brock's secretary sat outside in a waiting area at a modern acrylic desk like the rest of the floor—and Flynn leaned against a sleek filing cabinet built into the wall.

The Maddox VP shoved away and clapped an arm around Jason's shoulders. "Walk with me. Let's grab some food, then head back up to my office."

Like he had a choice. Jason suspected that Flynn was about to play his role of good cop after his brother's bad cop. Except he got the feeling it wasn't a game so much as their natural personalities.

Jason walked with Flynn as he jabbed the elevator button for the fifth floor. That floor contained all the other departments: public relations, art, financial. The offices were smaller than on the sixth, but still modern with stark-white walls and acrylic desks. Flynn smiled and waved as he walked past the rows of cubicles, calling each person by name, stopping to speak briefly with a couple of employees.

Finally they reached the large lunchroom with its modern kitchen. Brock Maddox kept the fridge well stocked, realizing that creative types enjoyed snacks while brainstorming in one of the soundproofed breakout rooms.

Flynn opened the fridge and pulled out a sack of Chinese food. "There's enough to share. Do you want water or soda?"

"Water, thanks."

Flynn's approach was definitely more laid-back than that of his brother, who didn't so much as offer a chair, much less a causal walk around followed by food. They took a service elevator back up to the sixth floor, making tracks to Flynn's office. The space used to be Brock's from back when their father was alive, but Flynn had made it his own, much homier than Brock's current digs. Airy with live plants, a glass desk and several cream-colored sofas for impromptu meetings.

Just the sort of place Lauren would like.

God, did all roads lead back to her now? Would it always be that way for him? He needed to get over it fast, because she would be gone when he returned home tonight.

Maybe he would stay at the office and sleep on his sofa rather than torment himself with the scent of her lingering on his sheets. He would throw himself into work and salvage his career.

Flynn sat behind his desk and gestured for Jason to sit across from him. He passed a carton of sweet-and-sour chicken and a pair of chopsticks. "How are you holding up after the ass chewing from my brother?"

"He has a right to be pissed. It's going to take some masterful manipulation and a dash of luck to pull off the meeting with Walter Prentice this afternoon."

Flynn stirred the wooden sticks through his food. "Brock can come off pretty harsh sometimes, but it's because he lives for this place. He worshippped our father. He's determined to keep his legacy alive through the business. MC is his life. I don't agree with his way, but I understand." Flynn swung his feet up on the desk, unwrapping an egg roll. "I have what he calls a lackadaisical attitude toward the company."

Jason twisted open a bottled water. His old man would have gotten along great with Brock. Brock would also be one hell of a tough guy to have as an older sibling, always walking around in his shadow. But even though things were strained between the brothers, Jason didn't intend to risk siding with one or the other either way. Better to just let Flynn play out whatever it was he wanted to say.

Flynn finished off the egg roll in two bites. "Things are tight all the way around, but the business is basically secure. There's no cause for concern. Once we knock Koteas off his pedestal, we'll have a lock on this sector of the country."

"Okay, then." That wasn't the picture Brock had painted, but then, the Maddox brothers rarely got along smoothly.

"The tension between me and Brock is that obvious, huh?"

Jason shrugged noncommittally, swigging back his water.

"Brock and I need to work on not letting that show. Bad for business to put up anything other than a unified front." Flynn swung his feet back to the floor, leaning forward on his elbows. "I imagine you're wondering why I brought you in here."

"I'm the man of the hour." And not in a good way today.

Flynn's face went serious, tension making him resemble his brother all the more. "Let's put the Madd Comm crap aside for a second." He plowed a hand through his hair as he seemed to struggle for words. "Hell, I'll just come right out and say it. Don't let your work come before your wife."

Jason set his food aside carefully. That wasn't at all what he'd expected to hear when he walked in here, and he didn't know what to make of it.

"Lauren's heading back to New York this afternoon." He could already hear the empty echo of his house. He scratched under his tie, his chest going tight. "There are no other demands on my time." Not until the baby came.

"It's not too late for you, man. There're no divorce papers signed. Listen to me, I'm speaking from experience here. I let my family and my work come between me and Renee, and I've regretted it more times than I can count." More of that regret coated his voice even now. "Do you really want to end up like Brock? Breathing and eating the job so much he even lives here?"

Brock's primary residence was none other than an apartment in the Powell Street office building. A luxury setup, sure, but Jason preferred his house.

His empty house that wasn't even close to becoming a home until Lauren stepped inside with her ideas for filling it with furniture and plants. "It's all a moot point. She and I went into this with our eyes wide open. We were working some damage control of our own, trying to find the best possible solution."

"You're not even talking like the Jason Reagert we see around here. I can't see you giving up this easily."

What the hell did Flynn know? Jason had worked his ass off this past week to show Lauren all the ways their lives blended, the great life they could provide for their baby.

A whole week?

Damn.

Realization slammed through him. He didn't want to be *that* guy, the man who regretted not doing everything in his power to fight for the woman he loves. And hell, yes, he loved her. He wasn't emotionally closed off like his old man. His father would never have cared whether Lauren was happy, and his dad certainly would never have gotten choked up over an ultrasound photo.

A week might not be much time when it came to winning something as big as a lifetime together, but it was enough for him to be sure his feelings for Lauren were real. Lauren was perfect for him in every way, as a friend, lover, wife, mother of his child. He wanted it all with her.

Flynn was right. Nothing, no one and certainly no job should come between him and his wife. He'd be damned before he would let his life be dictated by business the way his father's was. He would follow Lauren all the way to New York, even if it meant starting up his own ad business there to be with her.

Once he finished his meeting with Prentice this afternoon, he would book the first flight out to reclaim his wife.

Lauren watched Jason's house in the rearview mirror as the taxi pulled away from the curb. Her suitcase was packed, her flight back to New York booked, her brief marriage over. She'd even gotten her wish for a no-scenes exit since Jason had honored her request to leave for work before she awoke.

Her life was such a mess she felt like a Picasso painting with her nose on crooked.

The city unfolded ahead of her, already crammed full of memories she'd made with Jason in only a week. Amazing memories. All those moments together merged in her mind in a bittersweet portfolio. She loved him, but didn't know how to build a life with him if he didn't love her back.

Her cell phone rang in her purse, jolting her. Could it be Jason? She fumbled fast to fish it out, read the screen. Mom.

Lauren considered just pitching the cell back into her bag. They'd talked just yesterday about nursery murals, after all, and she really didn't have the emotional energy to deal with her mother now. Except she was only delaying the inevitable.

She brought the phone to her ear. "Hi, Mom. What do you need?"

"I'm just checking up on you. How are you feeling?"

Lauren stilled in the taxi seat. There was a calm in her mother's voice she hadn't heard in a long while. Instinctively she flinched away from hope. Most likely her mother was headed for a downward spiral instead.

"I'm feeling a lot better these days." Physically, anyway. Her nerves and heart, however, were in tatters. "In fact, I'm ready to work at full speed again. I'm, uh, heading to New York right now to tend to some business." She would deal with explaining about the divorce later.

She waited for the sure-to-come advice and demands to spend every minute of every waking hour together. Her hand tightened around the phone.

"That's fantastic, Lauren. I'm glad you're doing well." Jacqueline paused, inhaled a shaky breath on the other end of the line. "Listen, dear, I have a specific reason for calling."

Lauren's stomach clenched. Here it came. Although you never knew what that something might be with her mom, except that it usually included high drama, a lot of tears and then lashing out. "I'm listening."

"This is very difficult for me to say, so please don't interrupt."

Lauren restrained a slightly hysterical laugh at the notion of her interrupting when most of the time she could barely get a word in edgewise. "Whenever you're ready, Mom."

"I went to see my doctor today. Not my GP, but my *other* doctor, the one I stopped going to a while back." Jacqueline's words picked up speed. "We've scheduled some follow-up appointments, as well."

A rushing sound started in Lauren's brain. She couldn't have heard what she thought. But she had. Hope was a scary thing. "That's good to hear, Mom, really good."

"Don't interrupt, dear."

"Of course." She shook her head, stunned at this turn of events. "Sorry."

"He also wrote me a prescription, some new drug on the market, and I'm going to take it. This isn't easy for me to do or even tell you, but I want to be the best, healthiest grandmother I can. I want to enjoy that baby you're having." Her glasses chain rattled on the other end of the phone. From nervous fidgeting? Probably. This was a huge step for Jacqueline, seeking help on her own rather than because her family pushed. "All right, dear, you can speak now."

Her mother had been in and out of a doctor's care before. Lauren prayed this new initiative on her mom's part would lead to a long-term healthy outlook. "I know how tough that was for you, and I'm really proud of you. Thank you for calling to let me know."

Never before had her mother discussed going to the

doctor, and of course privacy was her right. But she'd also expected everyone had to pretend the problem didn't exist.

That Jacqueline could talk openly about seeking help? Trusting in this new start would take a while to fully set in, but they'd taken a major first step today.

Lauren cleared her throat. "I love you, Mom."

"I love you, too, dear," her mother whispered, her glasses chain clinking faster.

The line disconnected.

She cradled the phone to her chest, trying to hold on to that tenuous new connection with her mother a little longer. She'd told Jacqueline she was proud of her, but the enormity of it rolled over her even harder now that she had time to process the surprise news.

Then she started to wonder. If her mother could be so brave in setting her life right, in taking control of her own happiness, why couldn't she? Lauren sat up straighter, the cell phone falling to her lap. She didn't want to leave San Francisco. She didn't want to leave Jason. She was his wife, pregnant with his child, and she loved him. Totally and completely.

Why was she running away from the promise of a life together? True, he hadn't told her he loved her, but had she even bothered to ask? Or told him *her* feelings?

She stared out the window at the town she was only just beginning to explore. An SUV packed with a family and pulling a boat passed in the other lane, reminding her of Jason's yacht and all the weekend trips they could take, trips she'd never let herself think about even though Jason had tried to get her to look beyond this week.

The cab passed a restaurant, and she thought of licking

maple syrup off Jason's body. A plant nursery brought visions of him helping with a garden. She saw possibilities everywhere. It was as if the cap had come off a genie bottle once she gave herself permission to think "what if," and now she couldn't get the genie back in. She was wishing for a future with Jason all over the place.

She'd only given their relationship one simple week. No time at all in the big scheme of things. Running away was a cowardly thing to do. How ironic to spend all her life trying not to be her mother, yet now, she knew, she had a thing or two to learn about bravery from Jacqueline.

Starting today.

Lauren tapped on the plastic partition between her and the cabbie. "Excuse me? Could you turn around, please? I don't want to go to the airport, after all. I need you to drive me to Powell Street. The Maddox Building."

Standing in the MC boardroom at the head of the table, Jason thought of that "damage control" speech Brock had spelled out.

And he couldn't give it.

If he wanted to win his wife back, it had to start now, even when she wasn't around to hear what he was saying. "Mr. Prentice, while I value having you as a client, there's nothing more important than Lauren and our baby. I would rather pass your account to someone else in the firm than let anything come between me and my wife."

Walter Prentice rocked back in the red leather chair, his eyes narrowed, inscrutable. "Do you realize, Reagert, that I might very well take you up on that offer of another ad exec? I don't much like people misrepresenting themselves."

A gasp sounded from across the room. Jason pivoted fast and found...

...Lauren standing in the open doorway.

Chairs squeaked around the table as the MC executive staff jockeyed for a better view. Surprise rocked Jason all the way to his Testoni loafers, followed by caution. Then he saw Lauren's eyes filled with determination.

"Mr. Prentice." She strode into the room confidently, sliding her hand in the crook of Jason's elbow. "I can assure you that Jason and I are in one hundred percent agreement."

Prentice's chest puffed full of bluster. "Are you planning to lure this bright young star away from MC and back to New York?"

"I have no intention of taking Jason away." She tucked herself closer to his side. "Mr. Prentice, my marriage is rock solid. Nothing will budge me from San Francisco or from Jason's side."

She sounded as though she meant it. If this was some kind of act to pay him back for insisting on the fake engagement in the first place... Then he looked into Lauren's eyes.

And he saw love staring right back at him. Relief rocked him so hard he damn near forgot about the other people in the room until Gavin coughed helpfully, tuning him in again to Walter Prentice.

"What about all these rumors I'm hearing about a marriage of convenience?" Prentice's face creased in disapproval. "Mrs. Reagert, did you really take a half-million dollars to pose as his wife?"

Jason wanted to tell the old guy it was none of his business, but Lauren squeezed his arm lightly in restraint. "Mr. Prentice, apparently it's no secret my business had a rough patch, and Jason was willing to do anything, absolutely anything, to help me. Just as I'm willing to do anything to help him. We're that devoted to each other's happiness."

All eyes moved back to Prentice. Everyone seemed to be holding their collective breath, too, because the room went completely silent while the clothing magnate mulled over Lauren's declaration.

Finally, Prentice threw back his head and laughed, the sound booming around the room along with all those hefty exhales.

Jason's included. Lauren was pulling this off. He'd been prepared to go to the mat for her, only to have her step in to fight for him. God, she was magnificent!

Prentice slapped Jason on the back, holding on to his shoulder with a paternal air. "I like people who live out my motto Family Is Everything. You're a couple made to be an advertisement for that."

The stunned look on Brock's face was priceless. No doubt he hadn't expected Prentice to be swayed that easily. Especially given Brock's personal motto had always been Company First.

"Maddox," Prentice barked, "give the newlyweds the rest of the week off. My orders. Surely there's some busywork for my account that the rest of your people can handle while these two start their marriage off right."

Everyone around the office table applauded and whooped agreement. Brock even clapped, albeit slowly. Lauren blushed but, man, was she ever smiling.

He rushed her out of the boardroom and into his office, slamming the door closed and locked behind them. Lauren's laughter filled the room, mixing up with his as he hauled her into his arms. He kissed her and she kissed him, no hesitation, no distance, just all-out passion and connection and relief. Knee-buckling relief that she wasn't leaving him.

Jason backed his seriously hot wife against his desk, an ordered day off sprawling ahead of him invitingly. But first, he needed to know. "Did you mean everything you said back there with Prentice?"

"Every—" she kissed him "—single—" she kissed him again "—word."

A sigh shuddered through him. "Thank God, because I realized today I can't let you go."

"Good thing I'm not leaving, then." Lauren tugged his tie, bringing him closer. "It's not exactly professional to make love in the workplace."

"We're married." The need to seal their newfound commitment surged through him. "It's not only okay, but completely in the best interest of my future success. Anytime I'm sitting at this desk, I'll be reminded of you, which will make me plow through work all the faster so I can get home to my family, to my wife, the woman I love."

Then tears filled her eyes. Her chin trembled; her smile damn near blinded him. "Well, then," she breathed against his mouth, "ditch my panties and get me on that desk."

"Keep talking like that and this time will go so fast, no one will suspect we've been up to anything."

"Since you never leave me wanting, I have no problem with that. We'll just get home all the sooner."

"Home." He tunneled his hands into her silky hair, growing longer and fuller, blooming like the rest of her.

"Are you sure you're okay with staying in San Francisco? I don't know if you heard what I said before you interrupted Prentice, but I told him I'm willing to move back to New York if that's what it takes to make you happy. I have the financial resources to locate wherever you want. I'm not going to lose you over a job."

He and his father had let work and prideful stands come between them. He wouldn't make that mistake again.

"Oh, Jason." Her voice shook, heavy tears welling up in her eyes. "I feel the same way. I realized I've been hanging on to an idea of success and happiness, limiting myself out of fear of losing control. Here, with you, is exactly where I want to be."

"You're more than I deserve." He hauled her against his chest, inhaling her sweet floral scent.

"Hey, you can keep right on romancing me to make it worth my while," she said teasingly. "Actually, I've been thinking. Why not take that money you dropped into my company and start a branch out here?"

"I like the way you think." He looked into her eyes. "We could work with each other again like we used to."

"We were mighty damn good together."

"Still are." And they would be in the future, as well. "You've always been incredible, special, but this week has made me realize just how much I love you. How much I need you in my life. I'm glad you decided to stay, but I would have come after you. I couldn't let you boot me out of your life a second time."

One of those tears trickled down her cheek into her smile. "I love you, too, you know. So much. The way you make love to me, the way you help me while making it clear you know I can take care of myself. I should have realized sooner, but I've been so scared. You make me lose control, you know."

Her hesitant admission slid a piece of the Lauren puzzle into place for him, making him see how her tightly controlled surface hid so much passion beneath. But knowing that—understanding her—would help him navigate their relationship down the road. "The last thing I want to do is frighten you."

"I've been running from the intense way you make me feel, so afraid that I'll turn out like my mother, that we'll end up like my parents. But I know better now. We bring out the best in each other."

And she was right. Only with Lauren had he been able to find the joy of a future and family he'd never expected. "Sounds like you did a lot of productive brainstorming in the past few hours."

"And I haven't even begun to tell you the plans I have for the gardens." Her fingers crawled up his jacket lapel. "Now that I've finished with business for the day…"

He lifted her onto the edge of his desk, in perfect synch with her as always. "It's definitely time for some recreation."

# Epilogue

*San Francisco, two weeks later*

Lauren Presley wondered how a man could be so deeply inside her body and mind at the same time. But no doubt about it, her sated, half-dressed husband, tangled up with her on the sofa, was one hundred percent emotionally in the moment.

She would make the most of a second go-round in their newly furnished living room as soon as she figured out how to breathe again.

The butter-soft leather of their burgundy-colored couch stuck to the backs of her legs through her thigh-high stockings, sweat still slicking her body from their frenetically passionate hookup.

Jason nuzzled aside her hair to her ear. "I have an idea. Let's break in every piece of new furniture this way."

She arched her neck to give him better access. "That could get a little tricky when that antique, upright piano you picked out arrives."

"We can just practice more of those inventive positions." He trailed a fresh bloom from the front yard over the swell of her stomach where their child grew, healthy and strong. "The flowers look great. I can't believe how fast this place is turning into a home."

"I'm only just getting started." She'd placed two topiaries by the front door and planted some cooler-weather snapdragons and diascia in the flower boxes, a nice beginning. But she looked forward to landscaping the garden in more detail over time. She had that now with Jason.

Time. Forever. Together.

She'd hired a full-time manager for her New York offices and had started the ball rolling for opening a San Francisco branch. Since she would soon have her money back, she and Jason had decided to use the half-million-dollar loan he'd given her as seed money for her expansion to California. It truly was a smart investment for their future and for their child. Lauren was already looking into plans for building an architecturally matching office behind the home.

Life was coming together perfectly.

She had her friend, her lover, her partner, her husband—and he also happened to be the love of her life.

They'd even invited her mother to come out and look at vacation condos for winter visits with her grandchild. Having Jason at her side made dealing with Jacqueline easier. While he still had a ways to go making peace with his own parents, she knew she would never be comfortable cutting her mother completely out of her life, especially now that her mother seemed ready to embrace help.

Lauren didn't delude herself. Dealing with Jacqueline would still be tough—to say the least—but she had a new level of confidence in her ability to avoid explosions by drawing better boundaries.

"Love you," she whispered against his mouth.

"Love you, too," he answered, and she never grew tired of hearing it.

Prentice's Family Is Everything motto was working well for them. Sure, their start had been for practical reasons, but they'd both been so stubborn and locked into their workaholic, cold lives, they'd needed a good shaking up.

Lauren shuffled, twisting around until she straddled Jason's lap. "I've got a hankering for pecan pancakes with lots of maple syrup. How about you try your hand with the basting brush this time?"

He stood, holding her in place as she wrapped her legs around his waist. "I say you are absolutely the best partner to work with, Mrs. Reagert. Absolutely the best."

\* \* \* \* \*

*Don't miss the next* KINGS OF THE BOARDROOM, *V.P.'S PREGNANCY ULTIMATUM,*
*available next month*
*from Silhouette Desire.*

*Fan favorite Leslie Kelly is bringing her readers
a fantasy so scandalous, we're calling it
FORBIDDEN!*

*Look for
PLAY WITH ME
Available February 2010
from Harlequin® Blaze™.*

"AREN'T YOU GOING TO SAY 'Fly me' or at least 'Welcome aboard'?"

Amanda Bauer didn't. The softly muttered word that actually came out of her mouth was a lot less welcoming. And had fewer letters. Four, to be exact.

The man shook his head and tsked. "Not exactly the friendly skies. Haven't caught the spirit yet this morning?"

"Make one more airline-slogan crack and you'll be walking to Chicago," she said.

He nodded once, then pushed his sunglasses onto the top of his tousled hair. The move revealed blue eyes that matched the sky above. And yeah. They were twinkling. Damn it.

"Understood. Just, uh, promise me you'll say 'Coffee, tea or me' at least once, okay? Please?"

Amanda tried to glare, but that twinkle sucked the annoyance right out of her. She could only draw in a slow breath as he climbed into the plane. As she watched her passenger disappear into the small jet, she had to wonder about the trip she was about to take.

Coffee and tea they had, and he was welcome to them. But her? Well, she'd never even considered making a move on a customer before. Talk about unprofessional.

And yet...

Something inside her suddenly wanted to take a chance, to be a little outrageous.

How long since she had done indecent things—or decent ones, for that matter—with a sexy man? Not since before they'd thrown all their energies into expanding Clear-Blue Air, at the very least. She hadn't had time for a lunch date, much less the kind of lust-fest she'd enjoyed in her younger years. The kind that lasted for entire weekends and involved not leaving a bed except to grab the kind of sensuous food that could be smeared onto—and eaten off—someone else's hot, naked, sweat-tinged body.

She closed her eyes, her hand clenching tight on the railing. Her heart fluttered in her chest and she tried to make herself move. But she couldn't—not climbing up, but not backing away, either. Not physically, and not in her head.

Was she really considering this? God, she hadn't even looked at the stranger's left hand to make sure he was available. She had no idea if he was actually attracted to her or just an irrepressible flirt. Yet something inside was telling her to take a shot with this man.

It was crazy. Something she'd never considered. Yet right now, at this moment, she was definitely considering it. If he was available...could she do it? Seduce a stranger. Have an anonymous fling, like something out of a blue movie on late-night cable?

She didn't know. All she knew was that the flight to Chicago was a short one so she had to decide quickly. And as she put her foot on the bottom step and began to climb up, Amanda suddenly had to wonder if she was about to embark on the ride of her life.

Copyright © 2010 by Leslie Kelly

Sold, bought, bargained for or bartered

*He'll take his...*
# *Bride on Approval*

Whether there's a debt to be paid, a will to be obeyed or a business to be saved...she has no choice but to say, "I do"!

# PURE PRINCESS, BARTERED BRIDE
by *Caitlin Crews*
#2894

*Available February 2010!*

www.eHarlequin.com

### HARLEQUIN® Blaze™

*It all started with a few naughty books....*

As a member of the Red Tote Book Club, Carol Snow has been studying works of classic erotic literature...but Carol doesn't believe in love...or marriage. It's going to take another kind of classic—Charles Dickens's *A Christmas Carol*—and a little otherworldly persuasion to convince her to go after her own sexily ever after.

**Cuddle up with**

# Her Sexy Valentine

## by STEPHANIE BOND

*Available February 2010*

## red-hot reads

www.eHarlequin.com

# HARLEQUIN Ambassadors

## Want to share your passion for reading Harlequin® Books?

### Become a Harlequin Ambassador!

Harlequin Ambassadors are a group of passionate and well-connected readers who are willing to share their joy of reading Harlequin® books with family and friends.

You'll be sent all the tools you need to spark great conversation, including free books!

All we ask is that you share the romance with your friends and family!

You'll also be invited to have a say in new book ideas and exchange opinions with women just like you!

**To see if you qualify* to be a Harlequin Ambassador, please visit www.HarlequinAmbassadors.com.**

*Please note that not everyone who applies to be a Harlequin Ambassador will qualify. For more information please visit www.HarlequinAmbassadors.com.

**Thank you for your participation.**

**Stay up-to-date on all your romance-reading news with the brand-new Harlequin *Inside Romance*!**

The Harlequin *Inside Romance* is a **FREE** quarterly newsletter highlighting our upcoming series releases and promotions!

**Click on the *Inside Romance* link on the front page of www.eHarlequin.com or e-mail us at InsideRomance@Harlequin.ca to sign up to receive your FREE newsletter today!**

---

You can also subscribe by writing to us at: HARLEQUIN BOOKS
Attention: Customer Service Department
P.O. Box 9057, Buffalo, NY 14269-9057

*Please allow 4-6 weeks for delivery of the first issue by mail.*

# HARLEQUIN® HISTORICAL:
## Where love is timeless

From chivalrous knights to roguish rakes, look for the variety Harlequin® Historical has to offer every month.

**www.eHarlequin.com**

PREGNANT BRIDES

*Inexperienced and expecting,
they're forced to marry!*

Bestselling Harlequin Presents author

# Lynne Graham

brings you the second story
in this exciting new trilogy:

## RUTHLESS MAGNATE, CONVENIENT WIFE
#2892
*Available February 2010*

Also look for

## GREEK TYCOON, INEXPERIENCED MISTRESS
#2900
*Available March 2010*

www.eHarlequin.com

# REQUEST YOUR FREE BOOKS!

**2 FREE NOVELS PLUS 2 FREE GIFTS!**

### Passionate, Powerful, Provocative!

**YES!** Please send me 2 FREE Silhouette Desire® novels and my 2 FREE gifts (gifts are worth about $10). After receiving them, if I don't wish to receive any more books, I can return the shipping statement marked "cancel." If I don't cancel, I will receive 6 brand-new novels every month and be billed just $4.05 per book in the U.S. or $4.74 per book in Canada. That's a saving of almost 15% off the cover price! It's quite a bargain! Shipping and handling is just 50¢ per book in the U.S. and 75¢ per book in Canada.* I understand that accepting the 2 free books and gifts places me under no obligation to buy anything. I can always return a shipment and cancel at any time. Even if I never buy another book, the two free books and gifts are mine to keep forever.

225 SDN E39X   326 SDN E4AA

Name _____ (PLEASE PRINT)

Address _____ Apt. #

City _____ State/Prov. _____ Zip/Postal Code

Signature (if under 18, a parent or guardian must sign)

**Mail to the Silhouette Reader Service:**
**IN U.S.A.:** P.O. Box 1867, Buffalo, NY 14240-1867
**IN CANADA:** P.O. Box 609, Fort Erie, Ontario L2A 5X3

Not valid for current subscribers to Silhouette Desire books.

**Want to try two free books from another line?**
**Call 1-800-873-8635 or visit www.morefreebooks.com.**

* Terms and prices subject to change without notice. Prices do not include applicable taxes. N.Y. residents add applicable sales tax. Canadian residents will be charged applicable provincial taxes and GST. Offer not valid in Quebec. This offer is limited to one order per household. All orders subject to approval. Credit or debit balances in a customer's account(s) may be offset by any other outstanding balance owed by or to the customer. Please allow 4 to 6 weeks for delivery. Offer available while quantities last.

**Your Privacy:** Silhouette Books is committed to protecting your privacy. Our Privacy Policy is available online at www.eHarlequin.com or upon request from the Reader Service. From time to time we make our lists of customers available to reputable third parties who may have a product or service of interest to you. If you would prefer we not share your name and address, please check here. ☐

**Help us get it right**—We strive for accurate, respectful and relevant communications. To clarify or modify your communication preferences, visit us at www.ReaderService.com/consumerschoice.

# Silhouette Desire

*Money can't buy him love...
but it can get his foot in the door*

He needed a wife...fast. And Texan Jeff Brand's lovely new assistant would do just fine. After all, the heat between him and Holly Lombard was becoming impossible to resist. And a no-strings marriage would certainly work for them both—but will he be able to keep his feelings out of this in–name-only union?

**Find out in**

# MARRYING THE LONE STAR MAVERICK

**by *USA TODAY* bestselling author
SARA ORWIG**

*Available in February*

**Always Powerful, Passionate and Provocative!**

**Visit Silhouette Books at www.eHarlequin.com**